AMISH APPLE HARVEST

BOOK #11 THE AMISH BONNET SISTERS

SAMANTHA PRICE

D1522541

CHAPTER 1

"Hmm, this is from Florence."

It was after breakfast when Cherish heard Levi's booming voice coming from downstairs while she was still upstairs in her bedroom. She wondered what he was talking about. *What was from Florence?*

She stopped brushing her hair and tossed the brush onto her bed, twisted her hair into a rope and hastily pinned it up, donned her *kapp,* and tiptoe-raced to the top of the stairs so she could hear better.

"From Florence? Are you sure it's not addressed to me?" asked *Mamm.*

"*Nee.* It clearly says Mr. Levi Bruner on the envelope, and all it says on the back of the envelope is that it's from Florence Braithwaite. No return address."

"That's because we know where she lives. Go on, open it and see what she says. I don't know why she didn't come here and talk to you herself. It's madness to send a letter when she's living right next door. Don't you think so?"

Levi was quiet for a moment. "It depends what it says."

"Hurry and look," *Mamm* urged.

"Give me a moment. Where's that letter opener?"

"I'll get it. It's got to be around here somewhere."

Cherish wondered why Levi couldn't open the envelope without an opener. Then, she recalled all the nicks and cuts on his fingers from something he'd been doing in the orchard. She didn't remember what.

There was some clattering and some banging, then she heard paper being ripped. After a few silent seconds, Levi said, "Remember the other day, Wilma, how we talked about selling the orchard?"

Cherish was horrified. Selling the orchard? Who did he talk with about selling the orchard? Not them. Not her sisters, and not herself.

"*Jah*, what of it?" *Mamm* asked.

"Typical," Cherish said under her breath. They'd

been discussing selling the orchard. That was something Cherish thought would never happen and it shouldn't. The orchard should've been passed on through the family through the generations. Not treated as something to sell like one would sell a used buggy.

Levi spoke again, "Florence is saying she and Carter will buy it if we ever wanted to sell."

Florence was inquiring about buying the orchard. If *she* bought it, then that wouldn't be too bad. Who better to take over the orchard? At least it would be run efficiently.

Then it was *Mamm's* turn to speak. After a loud scoffing sound from the back of her throat, she said, "They must have bags of money. They bought the Jenkins' place too, and I've heard it cost them a fortune for Eric Brosley to prepare the ground for them at their place, and for Eric and his men to plant their whole orchard. I heard that Carter didn't even lift a finger, and neither did Florence."

Mamm was hardly being fair. Florence had been pregnant back then and Carter was running his corporation. If they had enough money, why wouldn't they pay workers?

"*Jah,* but the Jenkins' orchard is small compared

to ours. Would they pay the kind of money we'd want?"

Irritation rippled through Cherish. Her father never would've dreamed that his beloved orchard would fall into another man's hands. And, Levi of all people—that was even worse.

"I'm sorry, Wilma, but I wouldn't sell to Florence and her husband. You don't think I should, do you?" Levi asked Wilma.

"Nee. Not likely."

Cherish was troubled when she noticed Levi had said, *he* wouldn't sell to Florence, and asked did *Mamm* think *he* should sell. He didn't say *we.* Had *Mamm* handed over the entire orchard to him? Was it solely in his name? No one had ever talked about things like that with her or her siblings. If it was true, it was a dreadful thing for the entire family. A true disaster.

"What are you doing?" Favor had crept up on Cherish where she'd been listening at the top of the stairs.

Cherish turned and scowled at her. "Shh. I'm listening in."

"To who?" Favor whispered back.

"Just be quiet so I can hear." Now they were both

crouched down listening to their mother and stepfather.

Wilma continued, "We should find out what this place is worth."

"What place?" Favor whispered in Cherish's ear.

"This place—*Dat's* orchard, our orchard."

"*Nee!*"

"*Jah,* now keep quiet so we can hear the rest."

"I'll come up with a plan," Levi said, "If I do sell, I'll need a place to put the money."

Cherish scowled. He was talking about the money that should be going to her and her siblings.

Favor nudged Cherish. "It's not his to sell."

"That's the thing. It might be."

"*Nee.* It wouldn't be."

"He's talking like it's his. How do we find out for certain?" Cherish whispered back.

"There must be some kind of paperwork around here somewhere, if it's official that *Mamm* signed it over."

"Good thinking, Favor. We need to have a look around when they go out, and see what we can find."

"*Nee,* that wouldn't be right."

Cherish frowned at her sister trying to be good. "That boat has already left the shore with things being done right around here. What's not right is Levi having anything to do with the orchard, so it's even worse if he owns it, don't you think? It should be ours. We should all own the orchard, or just *Mamm* should. What's it got anything to do with him?"

"Sounds like you dislike Levi."

"Of course I don't."

"Oh, Cherish, that's so sad."

"I said, I DON'T dislike him," Cherish hissed, still trying to be quiet so they wouldn't be overheard.

"I know what you really mean."

"No you don't. Not exactly." Cherish had no time for arguing, and why should she like anyone her mother married? It wasn't as though her opinion had been sought before her mother had married him.

She brought her finger up to her mouth signaling for her sister to be quiet. Then she noticed there was no more talk coming from downstairs. Cherish walked partway down the stairs, with Favor quickly deciding to follow, and they saw there was no one in the living room now. Levi and Wilma must've moved to the kitchen.

Favor and Cherish both crept down the remaining stairs, crossed the living room, and stopped out of sight at the kitchen doorway.

"I don't think it's a good idea to sell. What would

we do?" asked Wilma amidst the sound of clanging plates.

"When we visited the expert, my eyes were opened to how much work an orchard is. Particularly one like this, one of this size. It's not just work at harvest time. It's work year 'round. We haven't been keeping up."

"We kept telling him that," Favor whispered.

Cherish nodded to Favor.

"The girls haven't been out there every day collecting the windfall apples. They only do it when they feel like it."

"That's my fault I suppose. I'll have to keep on at them about it."

"You shouldn't have to, Wilma. They should do it themselves."

"Florence had to tell them every day and she checked on them to make sure it was done," *Mamm* said.

"I can't do it all, Wilma. Neither can you. You have the household to run. They're old enough to know their responsibilities and do their assigned chores without us constantly telling them. We'll have to work out what this place would be worth before we think about it further."

"*Ach,* good idea, Levi."

Cherish wasn't surprised that her mother's idea of moments ago had now become Levi's.

Then their mother and Levi went on to talking about something else entirely.

Cherish grabbed Favor's arm and pulled her out the front door, closing it softly, and walking until they were well clear of the house. "We have to tell Joy and see what she thinks."

"*Jah*, let's. She'll know what to do."

They hurried through the yard to where Joy and Isaac's caravan sat behind the barn. When they saw the door was closed, Cherish knocked once and opened it to see a very sleepy-looking Joy in her housecoat lying down on the bed. Isaac had already left for work.

"Joy, get up."

Joy sat up frowning at them, then stretched her arms over her head and yawned. "What is it?"

"Something dreadful has happened," Favor said as she followed Cherish in. Both girls sat on the edge of their sister's bed.

"Tell me."

They repeated everything they'd overheard.

"And, Levi says he wouldn't sell to Florence and Carter," Cherish said. "So that'll mean we'll all be homeless and the orchard will belong to a stranger. I thought it would stay in the family forever."

Joy frowned. "This isn't good. It's not going to be as easy as that horse we got Fairfax to buy when it was really for Florence and Carter. We can't do that with something as big as an orchard. When will he look for a buyer? Is he just thinking about it, or is he actively looking for a buyer right now?"

"Who would know with Levi?" Favor said.

"Favor's right. He can change his mind really quick. He said he wants to find out what the place is worth."

"Should we go see Florence and tell her of Levi's reaction to her letter?"

"Should we?" Cherish asked.

"It can't hurt and it might help them," said Joy. "Let's go."

As soon as Joy got herself dressed, the girls set off across the Baker Apple Orchard to the next-door property.

"I can't wait until Hope finds out about this. I wonder what she'll have to say about it." Favor tried to keep up with the others.

Over her shoulder, Cherish said, "She'd be just as upset about it as the rest of us. But we shouldn't mention it to Bliss because it involves her *vadder*."

"She'll find out eventually," said Favor.

"*Jah*, but we shouldn't let her know how upset it makes us. She'll get so worried that she'll need to talk with someone about it and that someone will either be *Mamm* or Levi. She has no other friends apart from us."

"And Adam," Favor said.

"*Jah*, the man she stole from me."

"Oh, Cherish," Joy said, "She didn't steal Adam."

Cherish closed her lips tightly together. Then she changed her mind. People should know the truth. "I know I did wrong and I confessed it to Bliss. Adam Wengerd only came back to this community because of the letter I wrote pretending to be Bliss. I was the true author of the letter, not Bliss. By the time she'd gotten around to telling him the truth, he'd committed himself to her." Cherish groaned. "It's a shame he's such an honorable man. He didn't want to hurt Bliss. And that's the true reason he's with her now."

"Stop it, Cherish!" Joy said. "That's not true. They are well suited and while the letter might've drawn him back, it was Bliss herself and her sweet nature that he fell in love with."

"And it serves you right too," Favor added. "Your

deception didn't work for you this time even though it usually does."

"Why are you two being so hateful toward me? It's so unfair." Cherish stomped ahead of them both.

Her sisters giggled at her, which made her even crosser. Once they reached the dividing fence between the two properties, Cherish had calmed down. She held the wires apart and each girl slipped through. Then Joy held the wires for her.

To throw attention off herself, Cherish brought up Bliss again. "It's weird how Bliss has got a close relationship now with *Mamm*. You'd think *Mamm* was her true *mudder*."

"And isn't that good?" asked Joy. "It's nice for her to have that relationship with another woman since her own mother died."

Cherish agreed even though deep down she was resentful of her stepsister's relationship with their mother. *Mamm* always blamed Cherish for everything bad that went on, whereas Bliss could do no wrong in *Mamm's* eyes. It just wasn't fair.

"Does Hope know about Levi wanting to sell the orchard?" Joy asked.

"*Nee*. I don't think so. We'll tell her when she gets home from work."

"Ach," said Joy. "She probably won't even care. All she's thinking about these days is Fairfax."

"Jah," Cherish agreed. "Fairfax this, Fairfax that. I wish Fairfax never lived next door."

Joy said, "You're only saying that because he liked Hope rather than you."

Favor giggled. "You threw yourself at him too, as well as Adam, and a few others that I won't even mention."

"I never did. Fairfax was just a friend. Even he'll tell you that. Sure, he's handsome, but I never said to anyone that I liked him. It's nothing like how I feel about Adam. I saw him and I put my claim on him and Bliss knew it. She was right there beside me."

"Enough nonsense talk," Joy said. "Let's just concentrate on why we're going to see Florence."

Cherish wasn't happy about keeping quiet. She was still annoyed by Favor's words. She had to put her straight. "Besides, Favor, Fairfax was an *Englisher* and why would I have wanted one of those?"

"He's not now," Favor said. "Well, officially, he won't be soon."

"Both of you be quiet," Joy said as they approached Florence and Carter's cottage.

"I think he's nice," said Favor. "Really nice."

"He is," said Joy. "Now, Cherish, when we get inside, you talk first. You were the one who overheard what was said."

"Okay. Carter's car is here. That means they're home." Cherish ran in front of them and leaped up onto the porch without her foot touching the two front steps. Then she banged on the door before she gave thought that baby Iris might be asleep.

Carter opened the door, looking at each of them in turn.

CHAPTER 2

"Oh, please tell me Iris wasn't asleep. We didn't wake her, did we?" Cherish asked.

"She is having a nap, but don't worry. That little girl can sleep through anything. Even you." He looked over her shoulder. "You're all here, almost."

"Only Favor and Joy. Hope's at work and Bliss is … somewhere. Probably with *Mamm,* bonding over visiting the ill or elderly, most likely."

Carter looked again at all their grim faces. "Is there something wrong?"

"Most definitely and it's regarding Levi," Cherish told him.

"Oh no. Come in." He showed them all into the living room where Florence had been having a rest while the baby was sleeping.

The girls ran to hug their sister and then they sat down.

"Would anyone like coffee? Or a cool drink perhaps?"

The girls refused Carter's offer of a beverage and then Florence asked, "What's going on?"

"You see, it's not very good, because ..."

"Wait, did Levi get my letter?" Florence asked.

"Yes," said Cherish. "And I heard them talking about it. Did you ask if you could buy the orchard?"

"Not exactly. I just wrote and said if they ever considered selling to let us know because we would be interested in buying it. That's what I said."

"Because then he started talking to *Mamm*. I know he's thinking of it. And worse, he spoke as though the orchard was his. *Should I sell,* he said. Not, should *we* sell."

Florence frowned. "I don't know what's going on there."

"That's the sad truth of it. Although it was our father's orchard, none of us has any ownership of it. Do you think he owns it entirely?" asked Joy.

"I'm not sure." Florence shrugged her shoulders. "Yeah, it could be true. Wilma might've signed it over, or he might be talking about it as though it's his because whatever he says will go."

"Since he's already wealthy, what would he do with his money after it was sold? He'd be silly to sell if he didn't need to, in my mind," said Carter who had taken a seat on the end of the couch next to Florence.

"He's got money?" asked Favor.

"I thought you would've known. That's the word on the street. He has a few houses and he's got his fingers into a few of the Amish businesses. Along with all that, I've heard he loans money to people."

Favor's eyes opened wide. "Like a bank?"

"Kind of, I suppose. Or a loan shark."

"Oh, Carter." Florence slapped him playfully on his knee and he laughed.

"I'm sorry. I didn't mean it," Carter said.

Favor huffed. "He's always saying we have to be careful with money. He insists we give him all our pay. Well, not me because I can't even find work. I'm too inexperienced they tell me, or I'm too young."

"That'd be just like him," said Cherish. "He's loaning people money that we've earned."

"How do we stop him from selling the place?" Joy directed the question to Carter.

Carter shook his head. "I think we can't stop him from selling if he's made his mind up." Carter rubbed his chin. "I don't know if I should've approached him rather than having you write the letter, Florence."

Cherish's face brightened up. "It would be perfect if you and Florence could buy it."

Carter's mouth turned down at the corners. "Like you said at the start, he wouldn't sell to Florence, and that means me too."

Cherish's shoulders drooped. "I don't know what to do. There must be a way you can get it."

"We have to at least try," Florence told Carter. "We can't just do nothing. Doing something would be better than doing nothing at all. Perhaps I should talk to Wilma. She did visit us recently. Barriers seem to be coming down."

"*Nee*," said Cherish. "It wouldn't matter if you made Wilma see sense in selling it to you. Levi wouldn't care what she thought."

"I'm sure he does," Florence said. "At least a little bit."

"Trust me. I know him better. He never listens to anybody. We have to make Levi realize it's a good idea to sell to you. Maybe if we get some people to offer him something really low for the orchard, and then you come in and offer him a normal price it'll look extra high."

"I wouldn't like to be involved in deception like that," Carter said.

"No," Florence agreed.

Joy shot Cherish a disapproving glance. "That's right. We can't be involved in anything like that, Cherish."

Cherish was upset. Now it looked like everyone thought she was bad. "Oh, neither do I, but neither is it right that he has anything to do with my father's orchard at all. He was my father too, Florence. You might've been special because you were the oldest daughter, but I was special because I was the youngest."

"Hey, I was special to him too," said Favor.

Carter put his hands up. "As a father, I know that each and every one of you would've been special."

"That's right," agreed Joy.

Florence nodded. "Let us think about it for a while, Cherish. I agree there must be a way but the right way will be something that won't keep us awake at night."

"I was just trying to help." Cherish pouted.

"I know you were, and we appreciate it." Carter smiled at her.

After Cherish breathed out heavily, she wrung her hands. "I was so upset when he said he wanted to sell, and it was good that you wrote that letter, Florence."

Florence smiled, knowing the orchard was always meant to be hers. That was just what her father would've wanted. He didn't put all the effort into it to have it be run down and sold off. "It's what I've always wanted since I was a little girl." Her best memories were of following her father around the orchard while he taught her things about the trees.

"If *Gott* wills it, you'll end up with it yet," Joy said with a nod of her head.

"Now, can we see the baby?" asked Favor.

"Yes of course. She's upstairs." Carter stood up.

"Oh, we don't want to wake her."

"You won't wake her, she's such a sound sleeper lately. Nothing like those first couple months. But you can look at her if you want."

"Yes please. We'd love to see her."

Florence took the girls up the stairs. Then she pushed the door of the nursery open.

Joy was first through the door, whispering, "Ah, isn't she beautiful, and look, she's still got the little blanket *Mamm* made her."

"She uses it all the time and she loves it. Obviously, she hasn't said that, but I'm sure she does."

"I just want to kiss her and squeeze her cheeks," said Cherish softly.

"You might have to come back another day for that. That will surely wake her."

"You're so blessed, Florence. Everything has worked out for you," Favor said.

"It has. Everything has."

"We should go home. We didn't tell *Mamm* where we were going and she'll be after us to do chores."

"It was nice to see you all." Florence walked the girls downstairs again where they all said their good-byes and promptly left.

While Carter moved to the kitchen, Florence sat back down. Her mind swam with thoughts of what the girls had said. She did have everything—a good husband, a nice little home, and a baby. Carter was well off financially and it seemed he could buy her anything she wanted. So, why was she discontented about the things she didn't have—really only the one big thing, the Baker Apple Orchard?

Why was it that she continued to look at what she didn't have?

Carter was the same. Every time he reached one goal, he was onto the next without stopping.

Was it human nature to never be satisfied,

ignoring the things in life that one had achieved to strive for what they didn't have?

If the orchard landed in her lap, would she then have her eyes on other things? Would it have to once more be the best organic apple orchard in the region, and then in the whole country?

If she was going to be like that she'd never be satisfied.

Florence made up her mind then and there to be grateful every day for what God had given her. She was truly blessed and she shouldn't forget it.

THAT NIGHT AFTER DINNER, Cherish spoke to Hope outside on the porch and filled her in on everything she'd overheard earlier that day.

Hope listened intently and then said, "That would be wonderful if Florence owned the orchard. Then eventually, Fairfax and I, after we get married, could help. We could both work for them."

"That's right, Fairfax could work on his old family orchard and you could work on *your* old family orchard. You would be the perfect people to work there. I'll be at my farm by then. I'm not going to be sticking around here. Not when *Gott* has blessed me with a farm of my own."

Hope gave a wistful sigh. "It would be really good if things worked out that way for Florence."

"How can we help it all happen?" asked Cherish. "There must be things we can do."

"Well, you can't force things. All we can do is wait and see what happens. And pray extra hard."

Cherish didn't like that answer. She was certain the sensible one, Hope, would've had a good idea. No one else had any, and Hope didn't either.

There was one thing for certain. Cherish was not going to wait around to 'see what happened.'

Nee!

Cherish was convinced that people made things happen in life, not circumstance or coincidence.

She had to come up with a plan. After she said goodnight to Hope, she left her sitting on the porch, headed up to her room and closed the door behind her. She pulled her chair closer to the window. This was her thinking place.

With her chin in her palms and her elbows on the windowsill, she stared up at the twinkling stars and the luminous moon. Tonight the moon was crescent-shaped, bright and beautiful.

It seemed useless to her to pray for Levi to sell

the orchard to someone he didn't care for. Prayers should always be possible prayers, she'd always believed. If Levi sold to Carter and Florence, that would be a miracle—like the crossing of the Red Sea on dry land, or the manna falling from heaven.

What chance was there of her seeing such a miracle in her lifetime? Were miracles like that meant for these days too, or were they only in the Bible days?

Levi didn't need the money, according to what Carter had heard, so the problem wasn't how much they could offer.

What would cause Levi to sell—to sell to Florence and Carter specifically?

Cherish's gaze dropped to the dark outline of the trees beyond the barn.

It was approaching harvest and perhaps a clue lay there. Levi had mentioned the harvest was a lot of work. Would that workload prompt him to sell? Maybe if there was another disastrous harvest, the value of the place would be destroyed.

Making him sell was one thing, but making him sell to Florence was something totally different all together. He would have to be desperate to sell to Florence. Levi had never liked her, and Cherish knew that from his face every time she'd seen him look at her oldest sister. Perhaps he still thought that Florence had stood in the way of Wilma and him being together.

After Cherish brainstormed with herself for half an hour, she saw her only hope was the coming harvest being a disaster. And, how would she make that happen?

Should she make that happen?

She bit her lip.

Could she actually do it, if she wanted?

CHAPTER 3

HOPE HAD a brief moment with Fairfax in the middle of her workday at the bed-and-breakfast. He'd been sent on some errands for his host family, the Millers, whose dairy farm he was staying on during his trial period.

Hope wasted no time telling him what was going on at her family home.

Fairfax took off his hat, and Hope noticed how much his hair had grown in the last few weeks. "There's always some drama going on with you and the girls."

"Hey, don't include me with all of them. This has nothing to do with me. It has everything to do with Levi."

"I hope he sells to someone who knows what

they're doing. Your father's orchard was always something my parents were in awe of and tried to emulate. On a much smaller scale of course."

"I'm not sure if Levi would sell, but one of the girls heard him talking about it. He must at least be seriously considering it."

"Perhaps he'd sell to Florence and Carter if he retained an interest? Like twenty or thirty percent."

Hope made a face. It was a terrible idea. "I don't know. I'll mention that to the others." She knew right away they would hate the idea. She knew they wouldn't want Levi to keep a share of the orchard. If he wanted out, they wanted him out completely. In fact, they wanted him out completely, regardless. She was positive that Florence wouldn't like the idea of Levi retaining a share, either.

"It was only a suggestion," Fairfax said.

Then Hope had a dreadful thought. What if Levi tried to change the name of the orchard to Bruners Apple Orchard rather than Bakers? She got a pain in her stomach and covered it with a hand.

He put his hand on her arm. "Are you okay?"

"*Jah.*" She dropped her arm by her side.

"You need a ride home later? I could come back after."

"*Nee denke.* I've got a couple more hours to do.

I've already arranged with Favor to collect me. I've still got some rooms to finish off. We're fully booked tonight."

"Booked full? Wow. Business must be looking up."

"*Jah*, we've always got people coming and going lately."

"Ah, that's good."

"If you think of anything else that might make Levi sell, will you let me know?"

"I doubt that I will think of anything. I'm new to the way Amish people think and how they do things."

"At least keep your ears open. You might hear something worthwhile." She and the girls needed all the help they could get.

"I don't think I will, but you never know. Gotta go—I don't want to be late getting back."

"*Jah*, you don't want them to report anything negative back to the bishop."

He smiled and gave her a wink. "I'll be all right."

BACK AT THE BAKERS' Cherish and Favor were

doing their afternoon chores. Today, they were weeding the garden.

"Things go so well for you all the time, Cherish. Everyone overlooks me and no one listens to a thing I say. I want to be more like you."

"You never will be like me. You're too soft. I don't care so much about things. Well, about anything really. I don't have much empathy."

"I can change. I'll lose my empathy."

As Cherish laughed, she retucked some strands of hair that had escaped her prayer *kapp*. "You're perfect the way you are. You shouldn't want to be like me or anyone else. You're you, and you should be happy with that."

"I'm boring." Favor pushed out her bottom lip.

"Who's said that to you?"

"No one. It's just how I feel."

"See, you're not boring or someone would've told you so." The truth was, Cherish agreed. Favor was kind of boring, but she had to convince her she wasn't.

"You're just saying that to make me feel better. I'm not perfect. No one cares about me and you always get all the attention."

"It's not good attention. I'm in trouble ... constantly."

"I know, but you always get what you want in the end. I was thinking about this last night. You behaved badly so you kept getting sent to Aunt Dagmar's. Then, Aunt Dagmar died and left you her farm—her whole entire farm. How's that fair?"

"I loved Aunt Dagmar and she loved me. That's why it's fair."

"*Jah*, but don't you get it? You were only sent there because you were bad. I behaved and didn't get to go anywhere. No one gave me a farm for good behavior."

Cherish pushed out her bottom lip and thought about what Favor said. "I don't see it that way."

"That's because you don't want to."

Cherish narrowed her eyes. She could see what Favor meant, but there was nothing that could be done about it.

Favor continued, "There's nothing to be gained by constantly doing the right thing. Last night, in the early hours of the morning, I made my decision."

"What was that?"

"If you do nothing, you get nothing. From now on, I'm going to be more like you."

Cherish smiled. "Is that what you want?"

"*Jah*, I just said it is."

"Okay, well, do what you want. I can't stop you or control you."

"I will. Starting right now. No one will expect it."

Cherish stared at her sister, one year older than she. What was she planning? Whatever it was, Favor was right—no one would see it coming. Not from Favor. No one expected anything out-of-line from her. "Anything I should worry about?"

"Nee."

"Gut."

Favor stood up and threw down her weeding tool. "I'm tired of this. I need to walk around because I'm aching from bending down."

"Me too." Cherish stood. "Let's go."

Favor took off and Cherish walked along, dragging her feet. "I don't know if we should leave the garden. Someone might look out the window and see we're not there."

"Come on, hurry up. Hurry or I won't tell you my secret."

That got Cherish's interest. She caught up to Favor. "You have a secret?"

"Jah."

"Tell me."

"How do I know if I can trust you with the secret?"

"You can. I told you I'll never tell Levi or *Mamm* or anyone secrets again."

"I do have another secret that I could tell you."

"*Jah,* do tell me. What is it? Are you in love with someone?"

Favor giggled. "I'd never tell you that, but no nothing like that. It's not my secret really, it's someone else's. I'd never tell you anything of mine."

"Who is it about?"

"Favor. Me."

"What did you do?"

"I invited Caroline to stay."

"What?" Cherish screeched.

"I've decided to invite Caroline to stay with us for the harvest. We always need extra hands and I'm sure Caroline will love it. She's invited me to stay with her millions of times and she's hinted at staying here and I never could get permission to invite her, but now I will just do it."

It was a dreadful idea. Even she wasn't game to go against their stepfather. In fact, those times she'd been sent to Aunt Dagmar's farm was way before Levi was on the scene. "Levi will never allow it."

"Once she's here, he'll have to let her stay and so will *Mamm*. It would be rude to turn her away. Besides, we'll be needing extra help soon with the harvest. I'll have her making the cider in no time. She can join us when we do the canning and preserving too."

"Hmm. There are so many jobs to do. Is she a city girl?"

"*Jah*, that's why she'll love the harvest time as much as we do. She's never even been to an orchard. She said the closest she's got to one is in the fruit section of a grocery store."

"Let me get this right. You're going to ask her to stay before you ask *Mamm* or Levi?"

"That's right. Even if they do decide to sell, they won't find a buyer before harvest. I'd be surprised if they do." Favor twirled her bonnet strings in her fingers. "Hey, where are we supposed to live when we sell? I mean, when he sells?"

"I've got no idea. Levi will probably have us cramped up in some three-bedroom dump of a house with an outside bathroom—just one of them. And he'll probably sell all our animals and leave us with one buggy and only two horses."

"*Nee!* Do you really think so?"

"I think he'll do that. What makes me really annoyed is that he's got plenty of money so what's he saving it all for?" Cherish shook her head in disgust. Then she looked up and saw Bliss running over to meet them. "Shh. Here comes Bliss. Don't let her know what I just said. It'll upset her."

"Of course I won't."

"What are you two doing?" Bliss said once she got close enough.

"We're pulling out weeds, can't you tell?"

"Hush, Cherish," Favor said, making Cherish feel bad.

When Bliss pouted, Cherish wanted to cheer her up. "Favor's inviting a pen pal to stay without asking your *vadder*."

Bliss stared at Favor while Favor's jaw dropped open with shock at Cherish revealing what should've been a secret. "Is that true?" Bliss asked.

"Yeah. Why not?"

"You'll get into dreadful trouble."

"*Jah*, well don't you breathe a word of it. I'm prepared to get into trouble. I'll take whatever punishment they give out. Once she arrives, they can't put her on the street. They'll have to let her stay."

Bliss giggled. "That's true. I'm excited to meet her. What's she like?"

"Nice. You'll really like her. I've never met her myself, but she's nice in her letters."

Cherish asked Bliss, "Do you think your *vadder*

will allow this *Englisher* to stay? Or will he send her back home?"

"I don't know. I really can't say. He's never been put in this position before. And why don't you call him *Dat?* I called Wilma *Mamm* even though she's my *stepmudder.*"

"I have one *vadder.* Levi is a man who married my mother. It doesn't make him my … He's not my *vadder,* let's just say that. She could've married the best or the worst person in the world and I'm not saying that Levi is the worst person in the world, but she could've married someone like that and would I call him *Dat? Nee,* I would not."

"Oh, I think I understand. It's not that you don't like my *vadder,* it's just that you wouldn't call anyone *Dat* even if you liked him?"

"That's right. You're not as stupid as they say." Cherish smiled.

"Wait, who says I'm stupid?"

"No one does, Bliss. She's just teasing you. Pay her no mind," Favor said.

"Don't tell anyone," Cherish cautioned Bliss. "Or you'll ruin everything."

Bliss frowned. "Of course I won't. Who would I tell?"

"Let's finish off here with the walking. I'm done.

I'd rather pull the weeds," said Cherish, turning on her heel.

Favor followed her younger sister's lead and started heading back too. *"Jah,* looks like we've done some good work there already. There's not a lot to finish up."

"And I'll help too," said Bliss, walking along with them.

CHAPTER 4

THE NEXT DAY, Fairfax made another surprise visit to Hope's work. Hope was supposed to be riding her bike home, but when she wheeled it around the corner of the guesthouse, she saw Fairfax's borrowed buggy. That meant he might be able to give her a ride home.

"What are you doing here?" she asked him.

He jumped out of the buggy. "Mrs. Miller gave me some time off this afternoon." He took the bike from her and put it into the back of the buggy.

"*Wunderbaar.* What are we doing?"

"She wants you to come to her place to visit with her sometime. She said for lunch, but that would be hard with you working six days a week, finishing at two each day. I told her that and then she said for you to come after you finish work. I get to collect you on that day too."

"*Ach*, that's so nice of her. What day is this for?"

"Any day you want. She said even tomorrow if you can make it."

They both climbed into the buggy. "I guess I should speak with *Mamm* and see what day I can get home late."

"Do you mind if I ask your mother? I'll ask since the invitation is directly from Mrs. Miller."

"Sure. Take me home now and after we find out, we can have some alone time."

He smiled at her and then took up the reins. "I like the way you're thinking." Then he moved the horse and buggy onto the road.

"Mrs. Miller must be happy with the work you're doing."

"I hope so."

"*Jah*, or she wouldn't want to see me and surely someone would've said something to you."

"They did the first couple of days. I couldn't keep up. Now, I've gotten into the routine of things."

"It must be hard."

"It is, but many things in life are hard. It won't be forever. I want to be back working on an orchard somewhere. That's where I feel at home."

"*Jah,* me too." While they traveled through the tree lined streets, Hope's mind drifted to her future life she'd have with Fairfax. They'd both been raised on orchards, so it made sense for them to live on one, manage it, and raise their family.

She'd loved that, growing up—the excitement and buzz at harvest time, the changing colors of the apple trees as they adapted with the seasons. The pink blossoms of the springtime trees, the shedding of the leaves in the fall, the blushing pinks and reds as the fruit ripened, and the delicate green leaves in the spring. Every season was a delight that brought a different kind of beauty.

Then it all came together in a crescendo when the trees delivered their fruit. The sun, the soil, the bees, the water, the pruning, all worked together to make a bountiful harvest that provided wages for many.

Not just for their workers and themselves, but all the people who made money along the way to the final sellers at the fruit stores and the markets.

"Things are working out well for both of us. You've got a good job, and the Millers are happy with me. So is the bishop, I hope."

"*Jah,* he would be. It's thanks to you I got that job with your aunt. She's so nice. I couldn't imagine working anywhere else."

He chuckled. "You'll have to leave one day. We'll have our own orchard."

"Will we?"

"*Jah*. That's what I want. If we believe, and trust, it'll happen."

Hope felt good about what he said. He had such faith already. Even she couldn't see how they could have an orchard when right now they had zero money between them. If it happened ever, then surely it would be a long way off.

That didn't matter to Hope. As long as she was married to Fairfax, she didn't care where they lived or what he'd have to do for a living. He got on well with the Millers, so he might even be able to stay working with them after his official time was up.

Fairfax pulled the buggy up at the barn, and while Hope got out, he tossed the reins over the hitching post.

They walked into the house together, and they found Wilma in the kitchen shelling peas at the table.

"Ah, Fairfax, no one told me you were coming. Sit down and I'll get you a cup of hot tea."

"*Nee, Mamm*, I'll get it," said Hope.

Favor breezed into the kitchen. "I'll do it. You sit down too, Hope."

"Okay, *denke.*" Hope and Fairfax sat opposite Wilma.

"Fairfax drove me home today."

"Weren't you working today? Don't the cows need to be milked twice a day?"

"They do, but I got some time off. We don't milk them all day. We do it before sunup and again twelve hours later."

Favor noisily filled up the teakettle with water. When she'd finished, Hope said, "Fairfax is here because Mrs. Miller has invited me for a visit after I get off work one day this week."

"Can I come too?" asked Favor, as she sat down next to *Mamm.*

"I think she meant the invitation only for Hope," Fairfax said.

Cherish walked into the kitchen. "Hello, Fairfax. Who only meant Hope?" She sat down with them.

"Mrs. Miller has asked that I come here and invite Hope for lunch. I told her that Hope works until two. She said for her to come after that so they can have hot tea and cake together."

"*Ach,* that would be splendid, and what day is this happening?"

"Tomorrow, *Mamm,* if that's okay with you." Hope said smiling. It was nice to be invited to Fairfax's

43

host family. It meant a lot to her and made her feel more grown up.

"It'll be a nice time for us all. Tell Mrs. Miller *denke,* and me and my girls will be there. I'll collect Hope when she finishes work and go straight there. That way you don't have to collect Hope."

Fairfax's jaw dropped open. "All of you are coming?"

CHAPTER 5

"*Jah*. I'll look forward to it. I haven't had a *gut* talk with Elaine for a long time. I'll make a strudel to bring. Cold strudel goes well with hot tea on a hot day."

"It hasn't been so hot," Cherish said.

"No matter. All the better to have hot tea on a hot day."

"What were you saying about it only being Hope?" Favor asked Fairfax.

"Nothing, nothing at all."

"Do I have to come?" whined Cherish. "No offence Fairfax, but I've spent too much of my life sitting in other peoples' living rooms talking about nothing important. I'd like to emancipate myself from that situation."

45

Wilma folded her arms across her chest. "How do you know the word 'emancipate,' Cherish?"

"Somewhere."

"Give me a straight answer for once in your life, would you?"

Hope wasn't happy about all this squabbling in front of Fairfax. Being raised an only child, he wouldn't be used to arguments like these. She wanted to disappear right then and there. If only she could snap her fingers and take both Fairfax and herself out of the room immediately.

Cherish wore her grumpy face, and raised her voice. "I hear a lot at the café where I work, from all kinds of people."

Wilma stared at her, obviously trying to work out if she was lying or not. "So, you heard it at the café?"

"I might have. I can't really tell you for sure." Cherish shrugged her shoulders.

Wilma narrowed her eyes at her.

"You might as well come, Cherish, if everyone else is," Hope said, trying to disperse the tension in the room.

The kettle whistled and Favor jumped up to make the tea.

"*Nee*, it's okay," Cherish said.

As Favor once again made a lot of noise, she said, "Cherish thinks it'll be boring and not important."

"What would be important to you?" asked Hope.

"Anything that interests me." Cherish leaned forward and grabbed a sugar cookie from the plate in the center of the table.

"That's a very selfish attitude," Wilma said.

"Too bad, cuz that's the only one I have."

Favor only half-stifled a giggle.

"I'll bake cookies tonight to take. Will that be all right, *Mamm?*" asked Hope.

"Of course, as long as you clean up your own mess I don't see that's a problem." *Mamm* stared at Fairfax. "How are you getting along with the cows?"

"I'm getting more used to them and the milking."

"It's a tough job."

"I know. I knew it wasn't going to be easy, but still, I wasn't quite prepared for it." He looked over at Hope and grinned.

"Anything for love." Favor giggled.

"Well, I'm certain the bishop's had a good talk with you about what it means to be a member of our community, hasn't he?"

"He has, Mrs. Bruner. You can be sure of that."

Favor placed the large teapot in the center of the

table and then put down a tray of cups and saucers. "Help yourself everyone."

"Don't interrupt, Favor. The bishop and the elders had a good talk with you, Fairfax?"

Fairfax nodded, but before he could even speak, Hope spoke for him. "Of course they would've, *Mamm*. He's been careful to do exactly what's expected of him."

"That's right, Mrs. Bruner. I've had quite a few talks with him and with them. I've always wondered about *Gott*. I've always known there was something beyond myself. When I met Hope, she told me so many things and what she said made perfect sense. I've learned so much. I wanted to get away from the world and all the bad stuff it has to offer."

"Time will tell if you can last the distance."

Hope looked at her mother, horrified. *"Mamm!"*

"It's true. There's no use looking at me like that. Many people have told me that the people who have joined us don't stay. Sure, they might last a few years, but then they leave. There was the Gibbons family. They had three young children. They left after three years. Hmm, three children and three years. Three can't have been their favorite number. Or, maybe it was."

"That's not true," said Hope. "Most people I

know of who have joined, have stayed. I've heard about people from other communities not just this one." Hope despaired of her mother's comments. This wasn't encouraging for Fairfax to hear. He would've felt doomed before he hardly even began.

Wilma wasn't stopping. "Name some people who've stayed."

Hope looked at her blankly, hoping her mother would stop this talk.

"*Jah*, that's what I thought." *Mamm* pressed her lips together, looking pleased with herself.

"I'm sure there's loads who have. We can't just think about this community but all over the country people would've joined us, *Mamm*," Cherish said, sensing Hope's discomfort.

Then Fairfax spoke up. "Mrs. Bruner, the bishop told me it's not just the people born into it. *Gott* calls people to him. He did it in the Bible too. Anyone who belongs to *Gott* finds their way to Him. They may be late, like me, but they get there."

"Well, the bishop would know I suppose."

"I think it's *wunderbaar* that you're joining our community, Fairfax. It shows how sensible you are and … and mature."

He chuckled. "*Denke,* Cherish."

"I agree with Cherish," said Favor.

"You always do," said *Mamm*. "You should think for yourself for a change and stop blindly following other people. The blind lead the blind, Favor, and they both fall into the ditch."

"Ach, that's not very nice to say about blind people," Cherish told her mother.

"It's not meant to be real. It's meant as a parable, a story to show someone what's really right and wrong." Wilma poured the tea from the teapot into the cups.

"That's good because even I know it's madness for a blind person to try to show another blind person the way."

"I'm glad you said that, Cherish." *Mamm* put the teapot down and proceeded to pass cups to everyone. "Because that is what happens when your *schweschder* follows your example."

Cherish was shocked, but Favor smiled as though she wasn't bothered by her mother's words. "I am who I am, and I do what I do."

"Only if what you *do* is allowable by me and Levi." *Mamm* shook her head without taking her disapproving gaze off her second youngest. "What you just said could've come right out of Cherish's mouth. You two are spending too much time with one another."

Fairfax pushed out his chair, and then rose to his feet. "I should go. They'll have more things for me to do when I get back."

"They're called chores," *Mamm* said. "Sit and finish your tea. Would you leave before you drink your tea if you were having it with Mrs. Miller?"

Fairfax sat. "I'm sorry. I didn't mean to be rude. *Jah,* chores." Fairfax smiled at his future mother-in-law.

"I wonder why Elaine wants to speak with us."

"Probably to let us know how well Fairfax is doing," Hope suggested.

"We'll soon find out." Wilma brought the tea up to her lips and took a sip.

Hope saw Fairfax staring into his tea and remembered he didn't care for hot tea lately. He'd become more of a coffee drinker. She quickly got up and made him a coffee and then passed it to him. A smile exchanged between them.

"You don't drink hot tea?" Wilma asked him.

"It's not a crime, *Mamm.*" Favor sniggered.

"I do prefer coffee. I'm sorry, I should've said."

"No harm done." Wilma leaned over, and pushed his hot tea over until it was in front of Favor. "Now you have two to drink, Favor."

"Suits me. I love tea. I would've wanted a second anyway."

Hope didn't want Fairfax to be around all the tension, but what could she do? And, Favor was choosing today to challenge *Mamm* in all kinds of ways. They couldn't get out of there until they were finished with their hot drinks. Hope drank hers as fast as she could.

"You're doing a good thing," *Mamm* said to Fairfax. "I don't mean to say that you aren't. I've been meaning to ask you, what have you done with my horse you bought from us?"

Hope's blood ran cold. This wasn't good. Fairfax had bought the horse from Levi, when all along the real buyers were Florence and Carter. Hope couldn't even look at Fairfax. Was this a test from *Gott?* Would Fairfax choose to lie, or tell the truth, revealing the deception that involved Carter, Florence and her sisters?

"The thing about that was ..." While Fairfax looked up at the ceiling searching for words, Cherish knocked over her tea and it ran all along the table.

Favor then jumped up and screamed. "Cherish, you got it all over my dress."

"Let me help." Cherish pulled the tea towel from under the teapot, tipping it, spilling that tea everywhere as well. Everyone jumped to their feet, and Wilma ran to find something to mop up the mess. "I'm so sorry. Look what I've done now."

Hope pushed Fairfax toward the door. "Fairfax needs to go now, *Mamm.*"

"I'll see you tomorrow, Mrs. Bruner," said Fairfax.

Wilma glanced up at them. "Bye."

"I'll walk him out, *Mamm.*"

"And, we'll all see you tomorrow, Fairfax," *Mamm* called after him.

"I'm so sorry about that," Hope told Fairfax when they were well clear of the others. "She was rude to you and I'm not sure why."

"It's all good. Your sisters were pretty entertaining, anyway. Don't lose sleep over it. I won't be."

As they walked down the porch steps, Hope asked, "What would you have said about the horse just now?"

"I was going to tell her that I left him on my old property and he's being looked after."

"He's a buggy horse. She'll expect you to use him once you get a buggy."

"Maybe I could save up and buy him from Florence and Carter."

"That might work. *Jah.* They wanted him to have

a good home and they would know you'll look after him."

"I'd have to buy another horse anyway. I don't think they really wanted him, as you said."

Hope grinned. "That's perfect. I only hope they agree to sell him." She put her arm through his.

He patted her hand. "Leave it to me. I can be very persuasive." When they reached his borrowed buggy, he turned to face her. "Mrs. Miller just wanted you there. Now I have to tell her it's the whole family, nearly."

"I know and I'm sure *Mamm* knew it too."

"It's fine. I survived it. I'll see you tomorrow." He got into the buggy and she stepped back. As he traveled down the driveway, he leaned out the window. After he looked to make sure they weren't being watched, he blew her a kiss.

She laughed and put her hand up to make-believe catch it in the air. Then he pulled his head back in the buggy and drove away. After Hope stood and watched the horse and buggy fade into the distance, she walked back inside to speak with Wilma.

"He's gone already?" *Mamm* said when Hope sat down again.

"*Jah.*"

"That didn't take long. I thought you'd have a prolonged lovey-dovey goodbye."

Hope ignored her mother's teasing. "*Nee,* just a normal one this time. *Mamm,* why were you being so awful?"

"What are you talking about?"

"You know very well. You were horrible, saying that he won't last in our community. It was so unkind, so uncalled for. Maybe you shouldn't come tomorrow if all you've got to say is negative things to upset people."

Cherish and Favor sat drinking their freshly poured cups of tea in silence.

"If I upset him, he's too easily upset. Perhaps you should find a man whose family is here in the community. Someone's who's not so easily upset."

"*Nee.* I'm in love with him and we're getting married no matter what you think. You didn't upset him, but I could see that you were needling him. You made him feel uncomfortable."

"It's just the way I am. I was only teasing him. I do that all the time."

While Wilma looked totally shocked at her daughter's accusations, Cherish agreed with Hope, "*Jah,* you were quite awful to him just now."

"Cherish—"

"*Jah,* I know. Go to my room."

"That's right. And don't come back down. Not until you can learn some—"

"Manners," Cherish finished off the sentence.

"Correct."

Cherish stood, and walked out of the room. One thing was certain, when she fell in love with someone, she would not bring him to the house. Her mother had been acting awful just now. Poor Fairfax. Cherish shook her head.

She stomped up the stairs making sure she was making as much noise as she possibly could, then she closed her bedroom door firmly.

After a couple of minutes alone, her door opened. It was Hope. "*Denke* for what you did just then with spilling the tea." Hope sat on the bed beside Cherish.

"That was all I could think of to do. *Mamm* and Levi would think so poorly of him if they ever found out about the horse incident."

"*Jah,* it would be a disaster. *Denke* for your quick thinking."

"You're totally welcome. I like Fairfax, always have. We were friends once even before you and he were boyfriend and girlfriend."

"I know. And I know you never liked him in *that* way."

A mischievous grin met Cherish's lips. *"Nee.* I should've though, because he is handsome."

Hope giggled at her sister. "That's why I need to marry him as soon as possible."

"You are, aren't you?"

"Jah, as soon as we possibly can."

"That's a good idea. Otherwise—"

Hope covered her ears. "Don't say it."

"I didn't."

"You were about to."

Cherish laughed. "Okay, I won't say it. I'll just think it."

Hope lay back down on the bed, and Cherish joined her. As they were side by side, Hope continued, "I know you don't want to come tomorrow, but could you? I need you there as a buffer in case *Mamm* does what she did just now."

Cherish let out a long drawn out sigh. "I hate that kind of thing. It's so boring and time wasting. What do I have in common with an old married lady?"

"Nothing, but you'll be doing me a favor. And, think about this. You might need a special favor from me one day."

Cherish huffed. "All right. I'll go."

"Good." Hope rolled over and gave her a hug. "I just have a really bad feeling about it. Ever since *Mamm* said she was going."

"I know, and who knows what she'll say."

"I'm worried she'll say some awful things about me or about Fairfax."

"And, she probably will, but what can you do?"

"Nothing. Nothing at all. Just repair the damage after." Hope groaned. "Or trust you to spill the tea at the right moment."

CHAPTER 6

THAT NIGHT OVER DINNER, Levi kept looking at Favor. Finally, he said, "Favor, I heard a whisper that you invited one of your pen pals to stay without asking me."

Favor looked directly at Bliss. She'd opened her big mouth. That's the only way Levi could know. She knew Cherish wouldn't have said anything because she wasn't new to secrets or new to how the sisters worked together. Then she said to Levi, "You told me I could have a pen pal to stay."

"*Jah*, but at a time that is convenient to us."

"And now is not a convenient time," Wilma added with a sharp nod.

It was typical that *Mamm* supported Levi. Her loyalty should've gone to her daughters rather than a man to whom she'd been married only a short time. "When will it be convenient?" She was guessing, never.

He ignored her question. "You must write back to this young friend of yours and retract your invitation."

Favor swallowed hard. "It's not fair. Cherish gets to go to the farm whenever she wants. Bliss gets whatever she wants, and Hope gets out of this place because she works all the time while I'm stuck here to do all the chores." Everyone stared at her, so she said, "Why can't I have what I want for a change? I'm not asking much and you said yourself, Levi, that the Bible says we should entertain strangers. She's not a stranger to me because I know her, but she's a stranger to all of you. Don't you know that Scripture in *Gott's* word?"

"We do, but since you can't quote the source, it seems like you don't," Wilma snarled.

Levi shook his finger at Favor. "Don't go twisting my words. I said you could but if you go ahead making arrangements for yourself that'll be the end of it, and you'll never have anyone come to stay."

"Don't you care about me? Don't either of you care about me or what I want?" Favor stared at Levi and then her mother.

Mamm shook a finger at her. "You're not listening to what he's saying, you silly girl."

"I'm not a silly girl. Why are you so rude to me? I'm just invisible around here. I would be better off if I'd never been born. No one would even care." Tears streamed down Favor's face. She jumped to her feet and ran out of the room continuing up the stairs to her bedroom.

A few minutes later, Cherish burst into her room to see Favor lying on her bed, sobbing. "What's going on with you?"

"It's not me, it's them. They're at fault. They're so horrible and mean to me all the time."

"I know exactly what you mean. *Mamm's* getting worse. She never should've married Levi. We'd all be a lot better off without his stupid rules." Cherish sat beside her on the edge of the bed. "It's just not the same around here anymore—that's why I can't wait to get away. One day, I'll be at the farm in peace and I'll be able to do whatever I want." Just the thought of it made Cherish feel good inside. "Ah, the peace and quiet of the farm, the animals to care for, growing enough vegetables and fruit for myself to live off. Very few annoying visitors. And, Ruth next door if I need company for a change. She's nosy, but she's nice."

"Take me with you?"

"Sure, when we're older. If I didn't have that thought of being able to escape this place I'd go completely outa my mind. I do like working in the coffee shop. I'll miss that. I already told *Mamm* and Levi that as soon as I'm old enough to live by myself, I'm out of here."

"*Jah*, me too. I'll come with you if I'm not married by then."

Cherish grinned at the thought of her sister being married. "Who would you marry?"

"I don't know. Maybe I haven't met him yet. He might come from out of the area like Mercy, Honor, and Joy's husbands. None of them grew up with their husbands."

"*Jah*, maybe. That's unusual though. Mostly people in this community marry whoever's here. It's more convenient. So … who would you choose if you had to name someone right now? Someone that you know."

"I dunno."

"If you had to say someone, who would it be?"

"Hmm. If I had to name someone …" Favor thought for a while. "It'd have to be Timothy Hershberger."

"Timothy!" Cherish screeched.

"Shh. Keep it down. You said I had to choose someone, so he's the one I'll choose if no one else shows up."

"Interesting. I never knew."

"There's nothing to know." Favor huffed. "Just forget I said anything."

"I can't now. The image is burned into my brain. You and Timothy, eh?"

Favor giggled and gave Cherish a shove moving her off the bed. "Who would you choose?"

Cherish sat back down and faced Favor more directly, sitting cross-legged. "No one from 'round here."

"You've liked a lot of boys from here."

"Bliss stole someone from right under my nose. I'm too young for all that yet, so they tell me."

"We both are, I guess."

Cherish smirked. "I know, but there's nothing wrong with being prepared. It's good for you to have a backup just in case a nice man never visits. It's not as though Levi is ever going to take us on a vacation like *Dat* used to do. Remember all the weddings we used to go to in Florida?"

"A little bit. You've always had a better memory than I have."

"It was good to get away. When we were away

from home, there were no chores. That's what I liked best. Now that we're older, we should be traveling to meet people."

"*Nee*, let them do the traveling. They can come find me."

Cherish smiled. "I like the way you're thinking."

"I can't believe what Bliss did just now."

"I know. Me neither. Doesn't she know if it's a secret you're not supposed to blab?"

Favor pulled off her prayer *kapp* and started unraveling her braids. "You tell her that."

"*Nee*. I think you should tell her."

"Why me?"

"You're the one she blabbed about."

"So?" asked Favor. "You're better at talking than I am."

"*Jah*, but you should do it. She'll think I'm awful."

Favor's mouth fell open. "It's okay if she thinks *I'm* awful?"

Cherish giggled and lay down on the bed and rolled over onto her stomach. Favor leaned over and smacked her on her bottom with her brush.

"Ow!"

"Serves you right."

Cherish sat up. "Okay. Why don't we both wait

until she's in her bedroom and then we'll go talk with her. I'll be there for support, but you'll have to speak up for yourself."

Favor started dragging the brush through her long hair. "It makes me nervous."

"You want to be more like me, don't you?"

"*Jah,* for sure."

Cherish smirked. "Well, you're gonna have to start doing the things that I would do."

"Okay. What would you do?" Favor asked.

"I'd confront her. I'd say, Bliss, in this family, we don't betray each other. A secret is a secret. I trusted you with a secret and you let me down."

"I like it. That's great. But, won't that make Bliss feel awful?"

"Exactly. That's what you have to do so she knows how upset you are."

Favor sighed. "It seems someone is always upsetting someone around here."

"I'll go down and help with the after dinner clean up. Then I'll come back here when Bliss goes to her room."

It was two hours later when the moment of confrontation arrived.

Favor said exactly what Cherish had told her to say. Well, nearly.

"You told him, Bliss?" Favor stood in Bliss's bedroom with Cherish standing behind her for support.

Bliss's mouth turned down at the corners. "Don't be cross with me. I've never been good at keeping secrets. I'm so sorry. If I could take it back I would."

Cherish stepped out from behind Favor. "*Jah*, but then you'd only tell him again because you can't keep your mouth shut."

"I know. You're right. I'm sorry." Bliss put her hands up to her face and burst into tears.

The way Favor looked at her, Cherish knew she was going to get the blame for forcing Favor to be harsh.

Favor rushed to console their stepsister. "I was just so shocked and hurt that you told him."

Cherish rushed to her other side. "Did you want to get Favor into trouble?"

"*Nee*. I don't know why I told him." Bliss continued sobbing.

Cherish put her arm around her. "It's okay. We were just shocked that's all."

"I'm not used to keeping secrets," Bliss said, and then Cherish wiped Bliss's tears away. Then Bliss added, "I have no siblings."

"You do now," Favor said giving her a squeeze.

"You have us," Cherish added.

That made Bliss smile. "I'm sorry. Do you both forgive me?"

"Well …" Cherish said, and then Favor dug Cherish in the ribs.

"We do," said Favor. "Now, let's put this behind us."

"And, don't ever do it again." Cherish patted Bliss's shoulder while Bliss nodded in agreement.

"*Denke.* You two are the best." Bliss sniffled.

CHAPTER 7

EVER SINCE HOPE had started work the next day, she'd been dreading going to afternoon tea with Wilma and the girls at Mrs. Miller's house. By now, Mrs. Miller would've known that Wilma and the rest of them were coming. It was so embarrassing that Wilma had invited herself and the girls. Fairfax had specifically said the invitation was for her—Hope— and for her alone.

It was so kind of Mrs. Miller to invite her to share a special time with her. The invitation was a way of the Miller's saying they were happy with Fairfax and his work there. It was one thing Hope had wanted to do without her family, but what could she or Fairfax have said after *Mamm* had invited herself?

Fairfax was trying to keep in good with his future

mother-in-law. By now he knew that getting along with Hope's mother wouldn't be easy and neither would it be easy to get along with her stepfather, Levi.

When it came to two in the afternoon, the end of her workday, she said goodbye to her boss and then proceeded outside to wait on the roadside for the family buggy.

It was ten minutes later when the buggy appeared over the top of the hill in the distance. She waited and waited for the slow buggy. Finally it pulled up in front of her.

"Are you ready for your date?" *Mamm* asked her.

Hope got into the buggy. "It's hardly a date with all of you tagging along. And it wouldn't have been anyway because Fairfax and I wouldn't be having a date with Mrs. Miller." Hope crossed her arms over her chest, still not happy with the way things had turned out. "And please don't say anything to embarrass me while we're there."

A giggle spilled from *Mamm's* lips. "What possible thing could I say to embarrass you?"

"Where should we start?" asked Cherish.

"And why did you change your mind about coming, Cherish?" asked *Mamm*. "I thought coming to Mrs. Millers was the last thing you wanted to do."

"I know, but then I thought it might be entertaining, and I get so bored these days."

"I hope it's not too entertaining. I hope it's boring and then none of you will come next time," Hope said.

"You think there will be a next time?" *Mamm* asked.

"I don't know, maybe not. I'm not sure how long he'll be staying with the Millers."

"He's still there, so that's a good sign," said *Mamm*.

Hope was glad her mother was talking a little more positively. Hope looked around. "Who's missing?"

"Joy didn't want to come. She's got other things to do."

"Hmm. It still feels like somebody is missing."

"There aren't so many of us now." *Mamm's* voice was quieter now.

"I'm here, that's all that counts," Cherish said with a laugh.

It wasn't long before the girls and Wilma were all seated around Mrs. Millers long cedar table with Mrs. Miller and Fairfax. Fairfax had been sitting at the table when they arrived, in front of cakes, cookies, and small triangular sandwiches.

71

Mrs. Miller pointed to the tea and coffee at one end of the table. "Help yourself to tea or coffee. It's all there along with the cream, milk, sugar and lemon."

"It all looks so lovely. *Denke* for doing all this for us," Hope said.

"I'm happy to do it. What would you like, Wilma?" Mrs. Miller asked.

"I might have a sandwich. What's in those ones?" Wilma pointed to one of the smaller plates of sandwiches.

"Fish. Tuna salad."

"Oh. I'll just have this one." Wilma reached for what was obviously a ham sandwich.

Some of the girls gathered around the end of the table fixing themselves hot drinks.

"This is lovely sitting at the table like this. I thought we'd be sitting in the living room since it's afternoon tea you've invited us for." Wilma said to Mrs. Miller.

"There are so many of us, I thought we'd be better off here at the big table where everybody has a place to sit."

Hope counted up the places. The long table would've seated twelve people comfortably.

Wilma said, "I didn't realize you didn't have

enough seating in your living room. This place is nearly as big as ours."

"We do, but not as much as here."

"I quite understand." When everyone was seated again, Wilma asked, Mrs. Miller, "Now, why did you want to speak with Hope?"

"I just thought it would be nice."

"Fairfax is doing okay, isn't he?"

Mrs. Miller smiled at Fairfax. "He's doing a *wunderbaar* job. We're all very fond of him here. We'd like it if he stayed on, and he's giving that some thought."

"Are you, Fairfax?" Wilma stared at him.

"I am. I don't like to rule anything out. I'm considering all things."

Wilma looked at Fairfax, curled her lip and then looked at Hope. "Did you know that, Hope? Did you know you might be marrying a dairy farmer? You'll have to consider being a dairy farmer's wife and what all that it involves."

Hope gave an embarrassed laugh. "I'm sure it will be fine. I'll be happy with whatever he wants to do."

Mrs. Miller smiled. "Has everyone got enough to eat?"

"I have," said Favor.

"Everything is delicious," said Cherish.

When there wasn't much talking going on, Wilma said to Mrs. Miller, "Do you know Bliss has a pet rabbit?"

Bliss straightened in her chair and her eyes grew wide.

Wilma looked at Bliss and laughed. "Oh, Bliss, you look just like a startled rabbit that's about to dart off being chased by a dog."

"You have rabbits?" Mrs. Miller stared at Bliss.

"I do."

"And she wants more. I told her no, it's just not a good idea. The one she had reproduced and she still hasn't found homes. Do you want one, two, or maybe four, from Bliss?"

"What are you doing with rabbits, Wilma?" Mrs. Miller asked.

"I'm not doing anything. I dislike having the things at the house. Cherish gave one to Bliss for a gift and then one ..."

"*Jah,* you said what happened," Mrs. Miller said. "That's what they do, you see. They're breeders like no other animal." Mrs. Miller continued, "We do everything we can to keep rabbits away from the farm. They burrow holes and then the cows step in them and can fall and hurt themselves."

"That's wild rabbits that do that. Mine are pets and I keep them inside."

"Half wild, at least," Wilma corrected her. "The rabbit got out remember, and that's how we got four of them."

Bliss just sat there looking upset.

"It's okay," Hope said quietly to Bliss, who was sitting next to her.

Cherish was upset with her mother. Had she only accepted the invitation to make all her daughters look stupid? "It was my fault about the rabbit thing. They are very cute though."

"It's not good to keep them. Just one rabbit attracts more and soon you'll have your orchard full of them eating all your apples and destroying everything in sight. What they don't eat, they'll tell their friends about and they'll all be back."

"They haven't eaten the apples. It looks like we're heading for a bumper harvest," Cherish directed that comment at Mrs. Miller.

"Ah, harvest time. I'm sorry, Fairfax, but you won't be able to take time off to help the Bakers with the harvest. You can do what you want in your spare time, though."

"I know I can't, but I will help them all I can when I'm not working here."

"Don't you mean the Bruners?" Wilma stared at Mrs. Miller intently.

They were supposed to be getting along with Mrs. Miller, not embarrassing her. Getting names mixed up was an easy thing to do. Cherish held her breath, hoping no one would get upset.

CHAPTER 8

Mrs. Miller swallowed a mouthful of tea and set her teacup down. "Oh, have you changed the name of the orchard?"

"Nee." Wilma shook her head.

"The girls haven't changed their last name, have they?"

"Nee," said Wilma once more.

"I meant he was going to help at the Bakers' orchard. I didn't mean to offend. The girls are still Bakers and the apple orchard is Bakers Apple Orchard."

Cherish did her best to stop smiling. She could see why her mother hadn't spent much time with Mrs. Miller. It was plain to see that the woman didn't care for *Mamm* one little bit. Neither was she intimidated by *Mamm*.

"We know what you mean," said Hope when her mother didn't respond.

Wilma popped the remainder of her sandwich into her mouth. When she finished her mouthful, she said, "I wasn't offended. Many people are confused because Levi's name is Bruner and the apple orchard has Baker in the name."

Cherish looked around at her sisters. Bliss had been sulking since the negative talk about the rabbits began. Hope was looking frustrated because everyone was there when the invitation was meant for herself alone, and Favor was busy enjoying all the food. As soon as Favor finished one thing, she reached for another tasty morsel. Then, there was Fairfax who'd seemed awkward and embarrassed since they'd arrived there.

Finally it was time to go. Cherish couldn't have been more pleased. Mrs. Miller hadn't looked too upset when *Mamm* had said it was time that they leave.

In the buggy on the way home, *Mamm* said, "I had a lovely time there, Hope. It was nice to get some inner view of what Fairfax is doing and how he's coping with his new life and such."

"I'm pleased," Hope said absent-mindedly as she stared out the window.

Mamm continued, "I think I would like to talk with Adam Wengerd's *mudder.*"

Bliss said, "I would love you for you to do that, *Mamm,* but she's not from this community as you know."

Wilma said, "I know she's not from here, but I did hear a whisper that she's going to visit."

"Are you sure?"

"What *mudder* wouldn't visit her son? I would visit my son if I had one."

Cherish frowned. "You have two, *Mamm.*"

"*Jah,* what about Earl and Mark?" Favor said.

"I meant my own sons, not my stepsons."

"When is she coming to visit?" Bliss frowned, obviously wondering why Adam hadn't mentioned a thing.

Cherish stared at Bliss to see if she was upset about her stepmother's comment. *Mamm* had just made it clear that she thought differently about stepchildren. Bliss hadn't noticed, it seemed.

"Now I have to meet her. I hope she likes me," Bliss said.

"You are a perfectly darling girl, why wouldn't she be pleased to have you as a daughter-in-law?"

Bliss giggled. "It's a little early to say that. I'm not even old enough to marry."

"Of course you are. You're plenty old enough."

"I always thought I would get married at twenty-five."

"No, that's way too old. You must marry before then," *Mamm* said.

"I think they should get married whenever she wants to," said Cherish.

"You think a lot of strange things, Cherish, so the best thing you can do is zip your lips."

"I wonder if she likes rabbits as well," said Bliss

Wilma chuckled. "I can't see that a sane person would like rabbits except on the dinner plate."

"Mamm, that's very insensitive," said Cherish. "You know Bliss would never eat a rabbit."

"When we get home, you can go straight to your room, Cherish. Your answering back has got worse. And I'm going to talk to Levi about a punishment."

"What's he going to do to punish me? Make me go back and drink sweet tea at boring old Mrs. Miller's place again while you embarrass the life out of us?"

"That's a dreadful thing to say. And I'll be telling Levi you said that too. That woman kindly invited us

all there and you say mean things like that about her
—and about me."

Cherish kept her mouth closed. She had never
wanted to go to Mrs. Miller's place in the first
instance. Not only that, the invitation had only been
for Hope. Now Wilma was going to repeat the
dreadful business again with Adam's mother and
embarrass Bliss.

After a few minutes, Wilma appeared to be in a
better mood. "I would like for you to meet Adam's
mother, Hope. Do you think that would be
possible?"

"I wouldn't know, *Mamm*," said Hope.

Wilma giggled. "I meant to say Bliss."

"I don't think so, *Mamm,* because she lives so far
away and she's got a lot of *kinner* to look after."

"Why don't we have Adam for dinner? I'll ask
myself."

"It's okay, I can ask him."

"If I can't speak with her, I would like to ask
Adam questions. It was so nice sitting down talking
to Mrs. Miller. It was like talking to Fairfax's replace-
ment mother. And I don't know why I didn't get to
meet his parents before they moved to Florida."

"They'll be coming back to visit," Hope said.

"They made sure it was okay to do that. They asked me that and all kinds of questions."

"That's good. I would love to talk with them as well."

The girls in the backseat looked at each other.

Each knew what the other was thinking.

They were all shocked at Wilma.

It was Cherish who said what the others were thinking. "Why this newfound interest in boyfriends' families?"

"I just want to get to know them. There's nothing wrong with that."

"It depends who you ask. If you ask me, I'd say it's weird and a little bit loopy."

"So I'm loopy now. Is that what you're saying?" *Mamm* asked, half turning around.

"Not really. I said what you did was loopy, not you yourself."

"You think you're clever? Well, you're not."

"I'm only glad I don't have a boyfriend. Then you'd want to scare his family away and probably him along with them."

Wilma gasped. "As soon as we get home, you'll—"

"Go straight to your room."

"That's right. Not only that, tomorrow you'll be doing nothing but outside chores all day."

Cherish groaned. She wasn't prepared for that. Outside chores were harder than inside ones. That got Cherish thinking about her farm. She hadn't heard from Malachi, the young man who managed her farm, for a while. It was time to write him a letter. That's what she'd do this evening when she was banned to her room.

When they arrived home, Cherish hoped her mother would forget her punishment, but she didn't. Not only that, she was told she had to unhitch the buggy by herself and rub the horse down. Then do all the afternoon chores for the horses, including feeding and watering. The next day, she'd have to muck out the stalls, but she was trying not to think of that. It wasn't so bad.

Later that afternoon when Cherish was in her room and had just picked up a pen to write her letter, there was a knock on her bedroom door. "What?"

Bliss opened the door. "You have to have dinner in here tonight, *Mamm* said so."

"Good. I felt like being by myself anyway."

"Then after dinner, *Mamm* is going to fetch you to have a talk with her."

Cherish wasn't so sure about that. "That's something that's never happened. Is Levi behind this?"

Bliss shrugged her shoulders. "I've got no idea, but she was talking to him about extra punishments for you."

"I wonder what the punishment will be. I have to go to work the day after tomorrow. I hope they're not going to stop me from doing that."

"*Nee.* He would never stop you going to work. "

"Good. What's for dinner?"

"Lamb brisket."

Cherish turned up her nose. Her mother was always trying new things to force compliments from Levi and once she found something he liked, she stuck with it. "Not that again."

"It's yummy."

"I hate it." Cherish grimaced and then shook her head as though she'd tasted something foul.

"Be thankful we have food to eat. Many people don't."

"Send them the lamb brisket then."

Bliss backed out the doorway. "I'll bring your dinner up for you as soon as it's ready."

"Don't bother if that's what we're having. I'd rather starve."

The last thing Cherish saw before Bliss closed the

door, was her stepsister's pouting face. She put her annoying family out of her mind and concentrated on her letter. What was Malachi doing if he wasn't writing to her? She'd given him strict instructions to follow and that included him sending her letters with updates on what was going on with the farm.

Then Cherish started to worry that something was wrong until she remembered Ruth who lived on the neighboring farm. She was an *Englisher* who spent her time with her nose in everyone's business. If something was amiss, Ruth would've told her. Ruth even had the number of the phone in their barn.

No. There's nothing wrong.

The only thing wrong was that her hopeless farm manager was not following her instructions. She couldn't wait to rid herself of him.

Why was everyone in her life so annoying?

That night, Cherish fell asleep early. She woke the next morning to realize there had been no talk with Wilma the night before. Perhaps Wilma had peeked in her room and seen her asleep. Cherish decided to keep out of her mother's way today and maybe she'd forget about that talk they were going to have.

CHAPTER 9

WILMA DID FORGET about the conversation she was going to have with Cherish. It never happened.

Two days later, Wilma arranged to have Adam Wengerd over for dinner along with Fairfax Jenkins. She was still determined to get to know the families of the boys her daughters liked.

"Adam, Bliss tells me that your mother probably wouldn't be able to come here to visit us. She can stay here with us. We have plenty of bedrooms because this house used to house nine children. Their *vadder* wanted each to have their own space. The bedrooms may not be large, but we had one for every child. It's plenty big enough to have a few guests come stay."

Cherish quickly looked at Levi to see if he'd

minded talk of their father, Wilma's first husband. Since their mother had married Levi, they never talked about their father in front of Levi. Cherish wasn't sure why. Studying Levi's actions, he didn't seem to mind. He didn't even look upset. All he did was continue to enjoy the lamb brisket that they were having—again.

Adam swallowed his mouthful. "That's very nice of you, Mrs. Bruner, but I don't think my mother can get away from all her duties. They normally don't go anywhere."

"They? Of course she'd come with your father. Well, perhaps they should start going to places."

"Maybe, but they do have work to do, et cetera."

"What is this word, et cetera, that I hear people use?"

"It means, and so on, *Mamm.*"

Wilma's nose twitched in disapproval. "People only say that when they don't know what to say. Oh, I'm sorry I didn't mean you in particular, Adam. That was rude of me. But you see what I'm saying, don't you?"

"I do. I think."

"Tell me about your mother, Adam."

"What would you like to know?"

"Anything."

"I can't really tell you. She's just my mother."

"That doesn't tell me very much."

"She's kind, and very… she speaks quietly. I've never heard her raise her voice and she treats us all equally."

"Your brothers and sisters?"

"That's right. I'm the eldest."

"Yes. Bliss told me that you were."

"So that means you have been given a lot of responsibility," said Levi.

"I guess it does."

"It should make a man out of you."

"I hope so."

"So do I, for Bliss's sake," added Wilma.

Adam cleared his throat looking uncomfortable.

When Cherish kicked Bliss under the table, Bliss noticed how uncomfortable Adam looked. "I'm sure that your family is lovely, Adam."

"I'm not saying that they're not," said Wilma. "I just want to meet them. Is there anything wrong with that?" Wilma directed the question at Adam.

"No, there's nothing wrong with that at all. Not one little bit."

"Good. How are you liking your lamb brisket?"

"It's *wunderbaar.*" Adam smiled. "It's the best lamb brisket I've ever had."

Cherish exchanged smiles with Bliss. They both knew it was probably the only lamb brisket he'd ever had.

"It's *Dat's* favorite," Bliss told Adam.

"How is the harvest going to be this year? Will things pick up from last year?"

Levi's lips turned downward. *"Jah,* it looks like it's going to be good. Very good. I'm looking forward to a bountiful harvest if *Gott* wills it, and we've got a few surprises."

"What are the few surprises?" asked Hope.

Levi looked at Fairfax. "Do you want to know?"

"Jah, if you want to tell me."

"I will tell you one of them. The other I'm going to talk with Isaac and Joy about, privately. It's only to do with them and no one else."

"Tell us the other thing then, *Dat,"* said Bliss.

Levi smiled at his daughter. "This is just a thought, mind you. Ever since I married Wilma the girls have been at me to allow them to do a roadside stall like they used to. I didn't like them on the roadside where they're not protected. I can't stay there with them all the day long and they'd need a man with them. So, I've always said no. Then I thought it would be a good idea if we open the shop on our orchard again."

"That would be *wunderbaar, Dat,*" Bliss said.

Cherish was amazed. Had Levi truly thought they wouldn't be safe with their roadside stall? They'd done it for years and nothing ever happened. It made her think, though. Perhaps Levi wasn't all bad if he was thinking of their safety rather than saying no without any good reason.

"It sure would be," Hope said.

"That would be excellent because I'm ... Wait, but I can still work at the café?" Bliss asked.

"They said things would have to work out."

"He said he's only thinking about it right now," *Mamm* told Bliss.

"It's a good thought," Fairfax said.

"It is," Adam agreed.

"I think so too," said Cherish. "You were worried about us, Levi? Is that why you never allowed us to do it?"

"That's right," he grunted. "And I'll see what happens. I'll think it through further."

"Don't take too long. We'll have to see if it makes sense to do it or not."

"I don't see why it wouldn't make sense. It makes perfect sense," said Favor.

"Now we didn't have these young men here for

dinner so you could discuss what's happening with the orchard, Levi."

Cherish wasn't going to miss an opportunity. "Why did you have them here?"

"So we could talk about sociable things, things about them and not about ourselves."

Mamm turned to Cherish. "I think we'd all be a lot better off if you picked up your plate right now and finished it in your room."

Cherish's mouth fell open. "You want me to go?"

"*Jah.* Please. No one has a chance to speak with you around."

It was no time to argue. Not with everyone looking at her. She wasn't looking, but she could feel everyone staring at her. With her cheeks burning with embarrassment, she picked up her plate and walked to her room.

She hadn't even been talking that much.

Then she knew ... her mother truly disliked her. Perhaps Bliss had taken her place in *Mamm's* heart.

CHAPTER 10

"FLORENCE," Carter whispered when he quietly hurried down the stairs of their cottage.

She looked up from the home designs magazine where she was getting ideas for their new home. "What is it?"

"You'll never guess."

"Just tell me. What is it?"

"It's Wilma and Levi."

"Here?"

"Yes."

"Both of them?"

"Yes."

She jumped to her feet. It was mid-morning and she thought they'd have a quiet day, doing nothing. She wasn't prepared for visitors. Especially not these visitors. "What will we do? Will you answer the door, or shall I?"

"I don't know."

They looked at each other. "Maybe this is about the letter you wrote them," Carter suggested.

Florence gulped. "Do you think he's finally considering selling the orchard?"

"Surely not." Carter rubbed his jaw.

"I just wrote the letter not really expecting a reply."

"Maybe God thinks the orchard should be yours. He might've softened Levi's heart and given him another way of making money, then we can buy it."

"I hope so."

They looked out the window to see Wilma coming up the stairs, and Levi doing something behind the buggy.

"I'll get the door," Florence said.

"I'll hide in the kitchen."

In a flash, Carter was gone leaving Florence to open the door herself, a smile on her face. "Wilma."

Wilma reached the top step and gave her a smile back. "Hello, Florence." She held out a small package wrapped in brown paper.

Florence looked down at it. "What is it?"

"It's a dress for Iris."

"Oh, how lovely. You made her a dress? That's so nice and she's always used that blanket you gave her when she was first born."

"Good. I'm glad she's getting use out of it."

"Yes, she certainly is. Come inside."

"I can't. I have to go back and help Levi get something out of the buggy."

She stood on her tiptoes and looked over at Levi. "What is it?"

"Your treadle sewing machine. You see, I realized we still had it. Then I remembered you asking for it, and I don't remember what happened after that."

"Yeah, I thought about that, but it doesn't matter. You can use it." It was Florence's mother's but she didn't want to take it from the girls if they needed it.

"No, we're bringing it here for you. Levi is getting us another one."

Florence nodded. Wilma knew what it meant to her. "Thank you for bringing it to me. I'll have Carter help Levi."

Carter appeared behind Florence. "Hello, Wilma."

Wilma gave an embarrassed smile. "Hello."

"Did I hear that I'm to help Levi with something?"

"Yes, it's Florence's sewing machine."

SAMANTHA PRICE

"Oh, good. I was wondering how we could fill up the small cottage with more things."

He'd said it as a joke, but Wilma had no sense of humor. Florence hoped she wouldn't be offended.

"It was Florence's mother's," Wilma told him, clearly missing the joke.

"Good. Excuse me, ladies. I'll help Levi."

Florence watched Carter walk over to the buggy to join Levi who was maneuvering the treadle sewing machine out. It looked as though it could've been moved by one person, but it wouldn't hurt for the two men to do it together. They could talk and get to know one another better. They were neighbors after all and related through marriage.

"Do you want to see Iris? She's asleep upstairs, but you could peek."

"Oh could I? I'll be quiet. I won't wake her."

Spot was on the couch and opened one eye to look at Wilma, then he went back to sleep.

Wilma followed Florence up the stairs and Florence pushed the door open. Wilma walked past her and looked at the baby snuggled up in the crib.

"She looks just like Mercy did when she was this age. It brings back so many memories. They were the best days of my life, when you children were little."

Florence smiled as she leaned on the doorpost. It

was nice to see the softer side of Wilma. She so seldom showed it.

Wilma looked over at her. "She's precious."

"I know and she's such a good baby."

They heard the front door close loudly. "That'll be the wind. It always closes the door if it's been left open."

"I should go. We only came to give back your sewing machine. I think I can hear them downstairs."

"Thanks, but you could've kept it. Won't the girls use it?"

"*Nee*. Levi will get them another, as I said. Don't worry about us."

When Wilma and Florence walked back down the stairs, the first thing Florence spotted was her cast iron and wooden sewing machine. One of the few items she had from her mother. The other was the old photo of her, taken when she was a teenager and still an *Englischer,* that Florence had placed on the mantle.

Then Florence's eyes traveled to the doorway where Levi and Carter were talking.

Levi stopped, looked at Florence and nodded.

"Hello, Levi."

"Florence."

"It's good of you to bring back my machine."

"That's what Wilma wanted."

Florence gave Wilma a smile.

"And it looks good there," Wilma said.

"It does. I think we might leave it there. What do you think, Carter?"

"Perfect."

Wilma walked toward the door. "I won't keep you both. I'm sure you've got better things to do with a young baby in the house."

"Can we offer you some coffee?"

"No thank you," Levi said, as Wilma moved closer to the door. As soon as Wilma was out the door, Levi followed.

"Thanks for stopping by," Carter said.

Levi turned around and gave him a nod.

"That was a shock," Florence whispered when Levi and Wilma climbed back into the buggy.

"I know."

Out of the side of her mouth, Florence said, "What was he talking to you about? Did he mention us wanting to buy the orchard?"

"Not one word about it."

Florence was disappointed. "Oh."

"He just said our orchard was coming along

nicely. He was just making small talk, I'm sure he didn't really mean it."

Florence looked at her young orchard. It wasn't much to look at. "The thing is, he probably wouldn't know what's good or bad in regards to orchards. He doesn't know much at all."

"You're right. He could learn, but from what the girls have said about him, he doesn't seem all that interested."

They waved as the buggy moved away, and Wilma and Levi waved back.

CHAPTER 11

THAT AFTERNOON, Joy and Isaac drove to an address that Levi had given them earlier that day. They had no idea why they were meeting him there. He'd said it was important and Isaac had taken a couple of hours off work so they could meet him. They'd only just pulled up their buggy when Levi's buggy stopped beside them and they all got out of their buggies.

"How would you like to live here?" asked Levi as he walked over to them.

They looked at the house.

"That would be *wunderbaar.* Is it for sale?" Joy asked.

"*Nee.* I own it. The tenants have moved out and moved on. You can live here."

Joy didn't know what to say. They wanted to buy their own *haus*, not pay money in rent.

Thankfully, Joy didn't have to say anything. Isaac spoke. "That's nice of you, Levi, but we're well on our way to saving a down payment toward buying our own place."

Levi drew his eyebrows together, and then put a hand on Isaac's shoulder. He took Isaac a few steps away from Joy. "You've been saving for a while now. You'll want a home for yourselves and the *bopplis* when they come along. A proper home, not where you're living now in that small cramped space."

Joy could still hear everything Levi was saying. She didn't care where they lived. They'd make do until they could buy what they wanted—by themselves.

Levi continued, "I won't charge. Stay here for as long as it takes you to save."

Isaac rubbed his head. "That's generous of you. You don't want any rent?"

Joy was shocked at his nice offer, but she knew that Isaac wanted to be the one to provide for his family. Not wanting Isaac or Levi to know she'd heard the whole conversation, she looked down at the ground and traced random designs with the toe of her right boot, as though she was bored.

"It's generous of you, but you'll be losing money if we move here, and we've nearly got a down payment saved."

"You're refusing my offer?"

"I'm overwhelmed with what you've offered, but if we live here, it will be because of you and not because of me."

"I want to help you out but, if you don't want me to be involved, I can't. Why don't you ask Joy what she thinks?"

Joy was shocked. This was one discussion she'd rather be left out of. Of course it would be nice to live in a proper house, but it would be taking a handout from Levi. This seemed totally out of character for him. He was always doing things that were miserly and penny-pinching.

"I think … *nee*, I know Joy will be happy with whatever I decide. Same as you and Wilma."

Levi grunted. "Right. While we're here let's have a look through it, anyway." Without waiting for Isaac to answer, he turned to Joy. "We're looking inside the house." He walked ahead of them and opened the front door. Joy and Isaac looked at each other for a moment before they followed him in.

After Levi had showed them into the living room, he asked, "What is the difference if you live here or continue to live in that tin can that you're living in now? At least here you'll be more comfortable. Let a *vadder*-in-law do something for you. I didn't know Mercy and Honor well and Wilma and I won't be seeing their *bopplis* much. It'll be a while before Bliss has *kinner*. I just want to do something useful for the both of you."

Joy couldn't help wondering if there was some kind of catch. This was not the Levi she knew.

"Well, we could think about it," said Isaac.

"The other thing is, I am going to be selling it. It'll be too much money for the both of you, but I'd like someone living here while it's being sold."

"When are you selling it? We don't want to move around too much."

He chuckled. "I'll show you the rest of the house and you'll see why you'll be helping me as much as the other way around. Follow me."

When they'd moved into the hallway, he opened the first of the bedrooms. They saw at once the linoleum was rotted away, as were some of the floorboards. Some were so bad the ground underneath the house could be seen.

Joy couldn't help gasping. "There's a hole in the floor!" *So, that's the catch,* she thought, *and this is the Levi I recognize.* She wondered how Levi could have ever let someone live here, much less taken money from them.

"And one in the roof," Levi said as he opened the next bedroom door.

Joy cringed. "Ooh." She couldn't imagine having a baby in this falling-apart house.

The third bedroom, the largest one, needed just as much work done to make it habitable. It's window had a rotting frame and the pane of glass was cracked all the way across one corner.

Isaac folded his arms, looking deeply thoughtful. "So, what are you thinking, Levi? I do the work to fix the house in exchange for free rent until sometime in the future?"

Joy couldn't help thinking they'd be better off staying where they were.

"I'll show you what else needs doing first, then we'll talk." Levi went on to show them the rising damp and the leak in the bathroom, and informed them that the chimney was blocked. Besides that, the whole place needed new curtains, a sincere cleaning, and fresh paint everywhere—inside and out.

"There's a ton of work here, Levi."

"True. I'll pay for all the materials if you'll put in

the work. Then, when I see that it's all fixed, you can stay a further six months, rent free."

From the look on Isaac's face, Joy knew he was warming to the idea. It seemed a fair exchange and once the place was fixed up it would be a nice house.

"I'll give you a day to think about it, okay?" Levi said to Isaac.

"Okay. Joy and I will talk about it and we'll have an answer for you tomorrow."

The two men shook hands.

"*Denke* for thinking of us," Joy said as the men released the handshake.

"Stay as long as you like and keep having a look. I've got to visit someone."

They all walked out together, and the couple said goodbye to Levi as he climbed into his buggy. They waited silently until his horse and buggy were out of sight.

Joy looked at Isaac. "What do you think?"

"I could get some friends together and fix the place up in no time. You can collect some ladies to help clean. We'll paint it up, you can make new curtains and it'll look great. Then we'll also have however many months living here rent free. Do you know how much money we can save in half a year?"

Joy smiled at him. "We're paying nothing where we are."

"I am paying Levi a little."

"You are?"

"*Jah.*"

That was news to Joy, but it wasn't a shock. Joy then saw Isaac staring up at the house. "Looks like you've got your mind made up."

"Tell me your thoughts—I won't make a decision without your input, but here's what I'm thinking. It's not taking a handout because I'll be doing the work, but I still feel like we're getting the better end of the deal. It looks like a lot of work, but it's not. My friends and I can fix this in no time. Levi could've gathered people to help. He didn't need to offer it to us. He's helping us without us feeling that we're being helped too much."

Joy thought about what Isaac said. If Levi had offered him a good place for no rent, Isaac would've refused, but this way everyone was happy. "It was a good suggestion of Levi's and it was generous of him to think of us. I think we should take the blessings that *Gott* offers us."

Isaac stepped forward and hugged her. "I think so too. Let's tell him we'll do it."

Joy squealed excitedly when Isaac swept her off her feet and swung her around.

Suddenly, the door of the buggy swung open and Goldie jumped out. "Oh, Goldie. I forgot we brought you with us." When Isaac placed Joy back on her feet she leaned down and patted her dog. "We're moving *haus.*"

"We'll make the living room our bedroom until we get the main bedroom ready to occupy. But first thing will be to take care of the bathroom, and then the kitchen, I think."

"Sounds good to me. After all these months we've been living in the caravan it will feel huge, and even the lounge room by itself is bigger than that place. Not that I haven't been grateful to have our little home, Isaac, but I can't wait."

"I'm pleased you're happy."

"I am."

"Let's have another good look around this place. I'll take note of what all needs to be done."

They walked into the house with Goldie, and then Joy sat down on the only chair in the house. "I might have a little rest first before I go further." She placed her hand over her tummy. "I've been very tired lately. You have a look around. Don't find any more repairs than what you already know about."

Isaac laughed. "I'll try not to, but I will be looking hard so we don't encounter any bad surprises later."

"This will be our first home together with Isaac, Goldie." Goldie had sat on the floor beside Joy, laying her head on her mistress's lap. "It's not much now, but soon it'll be *wunderbaar.*"

Goldie licked her hand.

CHAPTER 12

THAT AFTERNOON, with Spot by her side, Florence was walking in her fledgling orchard looking at her young grafted trees. The baby had woken from her morning nap, 'lunched,' and now she was down for her afternoon one. Florence heard a familiar sound and looked up to see Joy pulling up in her buggy.

Florence was pleased to see her and turned to walk toward her.

"I have some exciting news for you," Joy said as she rushed to Florence

"What is it?"

"We've been made an offer from Levi."

Florence took a moment to let Joy's words sink in. Levi had left their place just a few hours ago, and they had expected Levi might want them to make *him* an offer—on the orchard. "What kind of an offer?"

"He's giving us free rent in one of his homes. We have to do some work on it—there are some serious repairs needed, plus cleaning and painting—and then we can live in it rent free for several months after it's all fixed up. That will help us save even more for a down payment on our own *haus*."

"That's wonderful news."

"I know."

Florence had half expected Levi and Wilma might offer Joy and Isaac a portion of their orchard property to build a home. Not all the land was usable for apple trees, and it was common practice among the Amish to do this. There was plenty of land by the roadside near where they had the shop. Florence thought it best not to mention it in case Levi hadn't offered. "Where is the house?"

Joy told her exactly where it was. "It's only two streets from where Hope works at the bed-and-breakfast. She could stop by after work. I could even drive her home some days." Joy looked at the young graftings. "They're coming along really well."

"I'm happy with them. They're all looking healthy."

"We've all got new beginnings. All my older siblings are married now."

"Except for Earl."

"Yes, apart from him. I wonder when he'll get married?"

"I don't know. I'm always hoping he'll move back, but I won't be holding my breath on that one."

"Me neither."

"Come into the house. I made some lemonade. It's perfect for this weather."

"I'd love some. Is Carter home?" When Spot licked Joy's hand, she patted him.

"He is. He's making a few changes to the plans we just got back from the architect."

They started to walk up to the house. "Oh, that's right. You mentioned you were going to build a new house closer to the road."

"That's the plan. Sometimes I don't feel like we'll ever get there. This is about the third time Carter has come up with some changes. He's a perfectionist. He likes everything just so."

"You'll be pleased about that when you move into your new house."

"I will. And I know he's doing it for us. He wants everything perfect for me and the children."

"'Children?' Florence, you're not…"

"No. Not yet. And hopefully not too soon. I'm still getting used to caring for one. Although, it has been good with Carter working from home. He's always there when I need help with anything."

They walked through the front door and just before they stepped into the kitchen, Joy stopped still.

Florence saw what she was staring at.

Joy said, "It's your treadle sewing machine."

"Yes that's right. I was quite surprised when Wilma brought it over to me this morning. Actually, both Wilma and Levi came—they brought it here together. They were both friendly and it was nice. I didn't mention the letter that I sent them at all, and neither did they. Not one word about it. But still they were friendly, so I said to Carter that this is a step forward."

When Joy didn't say anything further, Florence took a closer look and saw tears forming in her sister's eyes. "Joy, what's wrong?"

Joy shook her head.

"Has seeing the sewing machine here upset you?"

"Well that was in the Baker house forever. It seems like things will never be how they were. Now that it's gone and you're gone, things just aren't the same."

Florence put her arm around her. "Things never stay the same. Everything is always changing and so are our lives. Some things are better and sometimes things might get worse, but they balance each other out. And look at you, you're married now and someday soon I hope you'll come to tell me you and Isaac are going to have a baby."

Joy nodded, wiping a tear from her eye.

"Things are good for you."

"I know, Florence. I know they are. But it doesn't help when I think about how lovely things were and what fun we all used to have when we were children, when *Dat* was still alive. Mark and Earl were there too and so were you. You were like our *mudder*. It's just not the same since you left. You were the main person in the family after *Dat* died."

Tears stung behind Florence's eyes. It was true. She did feel like their mother. And she had been in charge of everything after their father died. "I get a little bit sad too when I think about times gone by, but in ten years or so we might be sad when we think about these times right now."

Joy sniffled. "Maybe."

"In a few years, you might have lots of children and then you'll look back and think how wonderful things were when you had loads of time to spend with Isaac."

Joy giggled. "I wonder what it would be like to have many *kinner*."

"*Mamm* had nine of us. Six of her own and three step children. That can't have been easy for her."

"And, yet I see things differently. I think things were easy for her. She's always had someone to lean on. *Dat,* then you, and now Levi."

"And there's nothing wrong with needing someone to lean on. I think everybody needs someone."

"Why are you defending her?" Joy stared at her.

Florence was shocked hearing that comment from Joy. "I'm not. Am I? I think I'm just seeing things from her point of view."

"*Jah,* I used to do that a long time ago until the scales fell off my eyes."

"Let's get you that lemonade. You might feel a bit better."

They walked into the kitchen to see Carter had the house plans strewn out across the large island countertop.

"Hello, Joy."

"Hi."

He started rolling them up.

"Don't do that on my account," Joy told him.

Florence said, "Leave it, Carter, it's okay. We'll get some lemonade and sit in the living room."

Carter looked over at her. "Are you sure?"

"Of course."

Joy looked at all the papers. "House plans?"

"*Jah,* and it's a never-ending project trying to work out what goes best where. The architect drew up the initial concept but we need to tweak a few things. I've got him coming back to go over some changes and additions."

"It should be nice when it's done."

Florence held up two glasses of lemonade and winked at Carter. "Let's go, Joy. Don't get him started talking about his plans unless you still want to be here at eleven o'clock tonight."

Joy giggled. "I'll just wait and see the end result."

"That's probably a good idea." Carter grinned at Joy and returned his wife's wink.

When Joy and Florence were sitting in the other room, Joy described the house that Levi had offered them. "At first I thought it was a bad idea, but then Isaac told me he could fix it up quite quickly. Then we've got all that time to save, and we'll be living in an actual *haus.*"

"Sounds like a great idea to me."

Spot jumped up on the couch between them, and then turned in a full circle a couple of times until he made himself comfortable, lying down and putting his head between his paws.

Joy stroked him. "Do you think we should do it?"

"I do. Why not? It seems you'll be helping each other."

"Good. We decided we'd do it, but I'm still glad to know you approve. I wasn't so sure at the start—I couldn't help wondering what Levi might be plotting —but once he explained everything it made sense and now I'm getting to like the idea." There was some other news she could tell Florence right now, but she and Isaac had agreed to wait a few more days before they shared it.

CHAPTER 13

A FEW DAYS LATER, Joy gathered her younger sisters into her caravan as soon as Hope got home from work. When they were seated on the bed and she was opposite in a chair, she began, "I've brought you all here today because I've got something to say and I wanted to tell you first, before I told *Mamm* or anyone else."

"Are you finally moving out of this steel trap?" asked Favor looking around to the sounds of Cherish's giggles.

Joy wasn't upset with her younger sisters and their rudeness. "Soon, but that's not what I want to say."

"Isaac's leaving the community, and you, for another woman?"

Everyone turned to stare at Cherish, who shrugged her shoulders. "Well, I don't know. If it's not that, I can't guess what else is so important."

"Are you pregnant?" asked Bliss, their stepsister.

Joy nodded. The girls screamed and ran toward her with outstretched arms, hugged and kissed her, nearly knocking her off her chair. She giggled. "Enough. You've got to be careful." When they all stepped back, she patted her stomach. "Careful."

They all laughed. "When is this happening?" asked Hope.

"I can't be sure, but I think around February."

"Oh, that's a long time to wait," said Favor with a frown.

"It has to cook," said Cherish, which set off another flurry of giggles.

Joy nodded again. "That's right and he or she is still cooking."

"I hope it's a girl. We have two nephews and only one niece. We have to balance things up."

"I'm hoping for a girl."

Cherish rubbed her chin. "I wonder if she'll be like you."

Joy stared at Cherish, the smile leaving her face. "What do you mean?"

"All good and proper like you, or will she be

totally different from you. Look at us, we're all different."

"She'll be just like me—even more proper." Joy's smile returned.

"What are you going to name her?" asked Bliss.

"Not Bliss," Cherish said.

Joy gave Cherish a frown, and then said, "I'm not sure, Bliss. I'll have to give it some thought, and of course Isaac will have ideas, too."

"And have you told *Mamm?*" asked Favor.

"Not yet. I might tell her today now that you all know."

"You'd better tell her quick," said Cherish giving Bliss a sidelong glance. "Some of us—well, one of us in particular is not very good at keeping her mouth shut."

"I'll be quiet about this," said Bliss.

"That's okay, Bliss. I heard about what happened and I don't blame you at all for telling your *vadder* what you did. I'd want my *dochder* to tell me everything too."

Cherish was shocked. "Even the secrets of others?"

"Most definitely, if it affected me or my family."

That wasn't what Cherish wanted to hear. "A secret is a secret."

"Well it looks like I better tell *Mamm* soon," Joy said.

"And *Dat,*" Bliss added.

Cherish immediately looked at Joy to see if she was going to tell Bliss that Levi was not her '*dat.*'

"I'll let *Mamm* tell him," was the nice answer that Joy gave.

"We'll be aunts for the fourth time. I'm so excited. I hope I will find somebody to marry," said Favor.

"Hey, I've been thinking of a way of getting Earl back here from Ohio," said Cherish about their half-brother. "Maybe we should match him with someone from this community and then he'd have no choice but to move back."

Joy shook her head. "I think he already likes somebody in Ohio, so that wouldn't work."

"If he hasn't married his 'somebody' yet, he can't like her too much," said Hope.

Joy put her hands in the air. "Hey, stop talking about him and start talking about me and this *boppli.*"

The girls giggled.

"Have you thought of names yet?" asked Favor. "Because I can tell you all the names of my pen pals. Some of them have lovely names."

"You name your pimples?" asked Cherish.

"I said, 'pen pals!'"

Everyone laughed and even Bliss's lips turned upward slightly.

Cherish made a face at her sister. "Stop going on about your silly pen pals all the time. I have pen pals too and you don't hear me talking about them all the time."

"That's because you don't care about yours as much as I care about mine," said Favor.

"Do too."

Favor pushed out her lips. "Do not."

"Do too."

Joy put her hands over her ears. "Right! Favor and Cherish, both of you can leave right now."

"Why us?" Favor asked.

"Because you're squabbling in front of the *boppli.*" Joy patted her tummy.

"He can't hear."

"I'm saying it'll be a she, and I can hear, so that means *she* can hear. You're upsetting me so both of you can leave right now." Joy stood and pointed at the door.

Cherish jumped to her feet. "It's a stupid caravan anyway. Who would want to live in a small and cramped place like this? Come on, Favor, let's go. We're not wanted."

Favor hurried to join her and when they were both out the door, Cherish wasted no time turning around and saying to Joy, "Are you still going to live here when you've got six *bopplis?*"

Then the door was closed in their faces.

"Oh that would've really upset her," Favor said. "You know they don't have enough for a down payment saved yet."

"How would I know what money they have? They could be squirreling it away somewhere for all I know and could have one million dollars."

They walked toward the house and Favor laughed. "It's your fault that we got kicked out."

"It was yours."

Favor gave her a shove. "You're arguing again."

"I'm defending myself." Cherish sighed. "Everybody's going ahead with their lives and I'm stuck here in this *haus.*"

"It won't be for long."

"Hope and Fairfax will soon be married, Joy's having a *boppli* and, who knows, Florence might already be onto her second. In no time Honor and Mercy will be onto their second child each, for their families and ... what have I got?"

"You've got a lovely farm and a job at the café. And you have a lovely caretaker named Malachi."

Cherish scoffed. "I have a caretaker, but lovely? I wouldn't be calling him that."

"He is lovely and dreamy."

"Dreamy! *Jah,* like in a nightmare—that's the only dreams of mine he'd appear in."

Favor giggled. "You're so funny, Cherish."

"Oh, funny am I now?"

"Jah, you are."

"Should we go back to the *haus?"*

"Nee, we'll have to do chores."

"We've got a lot of chores lined up to do. The sooner we get them done, the better. No one else will do them for us."

Favor sighed. "Okay."

CHAPTER 14

LATER THAT SAME AFTERNOON, Joy walked to Florence's house to tell her the baby news before Florence heard it from someone else.

"You're pregnant?" Florence asked as soon as Joy said she had news.

Joy nodded.

Florence screamed and then threw her arms around her. "This is the best news I've ever heard."

"Finally! I thought the day would never come."

They'd really only been married a short while, and Florence's thoughts turned to somebody who had been married for many years and was still childless. Then Florence realized Christina her sister-in-law would hear the news and fall into a pit of depression and self-pity. She had to visit Christina. "Who else knows about this so far?"

"Only the girls. I haven't even told *Mamm* yet."

"Don't you think you better do that soon before one of the girls lets it slip?"

Joy giggled. "You're right. I'll do that now."

She hugged Florence and then walked over to the small crib in the corner and kissed Iris on her forehead. "I hope I have a baby as adorable as yours, Florence."

"You will. She'll be adorable, just like yourself."

Joy swung around. "You think I'll have a girl?"

"Possibly. There's a fifty-fifty chance. Is that what you want?"

"I don't mind, boy or girl, but maybe I'm hoping a little more for a girl." Joy hugged Florence once more. "You've been the best big sister ever."

"Thank you. That's nice to hear."

"I'll go tell Wilma now."

"I'll walk you out."

Florence walked Joy to the door and then watched her walk away, slip through the fence that divided the cottage property from the Baker Apple Orchard, and then she was gone.

As Florence closed the door, she realized her child would not be able to associate with Joy's.

There was a gulf dividing them since Florence had left the community. It wasn't something she'd thought about when she left to marry Carter, but if she hadn't left, she never would've had Iris at all.

WHEN JOY HEADED to the family home rehearsing her words to *Mamm* in her head, she saw the front door open. It was *Mamm* and she had her hands up to her face. Then *Mamm* hurried over to her. From the look on her mother's face, someone had told her about the baby.

"Is it true?" *Mamm* called out.

Joy closed the distance between them. "Is what true?"

"You're having a *boppli?*"

"Jah, it's true."

Mamm smiled and Joy noticed tears of joy fill her eyes. "That's *wunderbaar." Mamm* hugged her.

"I know. I was just coming here to tell you."

"Bliss told me."

"Bliss?"

"Jah. Just now."

"Ach. She should've waited for me to tell you."

"It doesn't matter who told me. I'm going to be a

grossmammi again. I've waited for this, Joy, ever since you got married."

"*Jah,* me too."

"And, you'll have a proper home to take the *boppli* to when he's born. Thanks to Levi."

"I know. We're grateful." Joy couldn't believe how everything was falling into place for her.

CHAPTER 15

EVERYONE WAS HAVING lunch on Saturday afternoon when they heard a car pull up at the house.

Bliss jumped up and ran to the window. "It's a taxi."

Levi went to the front door, with the girls and Wilma close behind him.

"Who could it be?" asked Wilma, looking at the girl in jeans and a white shirt.

"Are we expecting anybody?" asked Levi.

"Nee." Wilma shook her head. "Not anybody like that."

"I'll go see." Levi walked over to the stranger as she was paying the driver. "I think you have the wrong place."

"No, the sign said Baker Apple Orchard and I'm here to stay."

Cherish looked on as the scene unfolded. It wasn't good. This had to be Favor's pen pal, Caroline, and she was chewing gum and wearing jeans, which were considered men's clothes and totally *forboden*.

Caroline ran a hand through her spirals of long blonde hair. Levi wasn't used to speaking to teenagers, not *Englisch* teenagers.

"You are here to stay, you said? And why's that?" he asked.

"Yes, I'm here to stay. I've been asked."

Levi screwed up his face. "Who invited you?"

"Favor did. She's my pen pal."

Cherish thought she could see steam coming out of Levi's ears as he huffed and puffed and then spluttered. "Wait right here," he told Caroline. Then he marched over to Favor. "What have you done?"

While Favor stammered and stuttered and Levi loomed over her, Cherish watched the driver unload two large suitcases and then he wisely wasted no time driving away.

Remembering she wanted to be more like Cherish, Favor pulled her shoulders back, took a deep breath and thought hard about what Cherish would say and how she'd say it. "I invited her. *Jah,* I did and I'm not going to ignore it. Ignore it? *Nee.* Deny it, I meant." She took a deep breath. So far she wasn't doing a very good job of her Cherish imitation. Cherish could speak much better than this.

"This isn't good enough, Favor. I'm surprised at you. You of all the girls, you have shocked me by this."

"I know I did wrong, but I am prepared to take any punishment you give me. Caroline has come a long way and we should be nice to her."

Levi put his hands on his hips. "I've got every intention of being nice to her, but I don't have every intention of being nice to YOU." He glared at her.

"What is going on?" *Mamm* hurried over to Levi.

"Favor has asked her pen pal to stay with us." He nodded to Caroline. "This young lady here."

"I thought this would happen one day. What will we do?" *Mamm* wrung her hands.

"We'll have to give it some serious thought. We can't turn her away. She's come from far."

"It's one of my pen pals, *Mamm.* Her name is Caroline. She's come to help us with the harvest."

Levi frowned, deepening the lines in his forehead. "Come to help with the harvest?"

"Yeah, we need help with that, don't we?"

"*Nee,* not from *Englishers,* unless we're paying them."

"She's an *Englisher,* but she's still a human," said Cherish, earning a glare from Levi.

"You know what I mean. Favor, you'll have to tell her to turn around and go home."

"I can't, *Dat.* She probably spent all day and most of the night traveling. She lives too far away."

Levi stopped still when Favor called him *Dat.* It was the first time any of his stepdaughters had called him that. Then ... then, his always-solemn face softened. It seemed he was pleased. It didn't escape Wilma's notice either.

"Perhaps she could stay for one night, or two maybe, until she makes the travel arrangements back home. Levi, what do you think?" Wilma suggested as the young woman walked toward them.

He shook his finger at Favor. "We will talk about this later. And what you did won't be without its punishments."

"I understand."

Favor smiled at Cherish before she hurried to meet her friend.

Cherish wanted to get to know the exciting *Englischer,* who looked so cool and confident. Maybe she could learn some things from her.

Bliss whispered to Cherish, "See, I kept the secret that she was still coming."

"*Jah,* you did and that means next time I have a secret I might tell you."

"*Denke,* Cherish, I'd like that. I can be trusted."

Everyone watched as Favor and Caroline hugged. Then she brought Caroline to introduce her to everyone. Once Levi said hello, he walked forward to carry her two large pieces of luggage into the house.

"You must be hungry," Wilma said to her.

"I am a little."

"Bliss, set another place." Then she said to Caroline, "We were just having the midday meal. There's plenty for everyone."

"Thank you, Mrs. Bruner." Then she turned around to see where her bags were and saw Levi struggling with them toward the house. "Oh, Mr. Bruner, you are so kind to do that for me. They are so heavy."

Levi smiled at her appreciation, and then straightened up. "They're not so heavy. We'll have a room made up for you in no time, Caroline."

"No need, *Dat.* She'll be staying in my room," Favor said.

Levi smiled once more at being called *Dat* by Favor.

With Caroline's good manners, Cherish guessed that Levi and Wilma would allow her to stay. And, it was a good thing that she'd suggested to Favor she use this opportunity to call their stepfather *Dat*.

Caroline moved into the house with *Mamm*, and Cherish noticed Levi glaring at her.

"I had nothing to do with it, before you say anything."

"I didn't say that you did."

Cherish was relieved. "Good, because I never know when I'm gonna get the blame about things."

"Still, who encouraged your sister to do this?"

"Not me, that is for sure and for certain. Why would I want Favor to get into trouble? I get the blame for everything around here."

Bliss said, "She seems a lovely girl and Favor did say she could stay. It's not Caroline's fault. Is there any real harm done if she stays? I mean, you can't say she'll be a bad influence. They've been exchanging letters for ten years or something like that. She can help with the harvest. We can put her to work. It'll be a free worker."

"It won't be free if we have to feed her. Food's not free."

Cherish moved closer to Levi and lowered her

voice, "Did you get a look at her. She's a stick. She won't eat much."

"I know how much you girls can eat when you're growing. It's a lot."

"*Jah,* but that'll be offset with all the work she'll do around here."

Levi dumped the two cases down to stroke his graying beard as his eyes glazed over. "She'd have to do a lot."

"And she would, she will."

"*Jah,* and how do you know that Caroline might not join us one day?" Bliss said.

"Does she want to join us?"

"I don't know but it might help Favor," said Cherish. "I can see how much she's hurting."

"Why is she hurting?" Levi asked.

"She sees what a lovely relationship you have with Bliss and she misses her *vadder.*"

"Ah, we do have a good relationship." He smiled at Bliss.

Cherish added, "And one that would be envied by many *vadders* and *dochders.*"

Levi laughed. "You are very good at getting your own way, Cherish."

"Does that mean she can stay?" Bliss asked.

"Just for the night and then we will see what we can do."

Before she could stop herself, Cherish jumped forward and excitedly kissed Levi on his cheek. "Oh, I'm so sorry." She stepped back, wide-eyed.

He chuckled. "That's quite alright. No real harm done."

"Can I tell the others?" Bliss said. "It won't be a secret if I'm allowed to tell."

"And, she will have to come to the meeting with us tomorrow," Cherish said.

As soon as he nodded, Cherish and Bliss ran to join the others in the kitchen. Levi picked up the bags and took them, one at a time, up the stairs to Favor's bedroom before he joined the women in the kitchen to finish off his midday meal.

When Favor heard the news, she was pleased. Her plan had worked. If Caroline was expected to go to their Sunday meeting, they'd have no time tomorrow to arrange for her to leave. That meant Caroline would be staying for two nights at the very least.

CHAPTER 16

Ever since Florence had heard about Joy being pregnant, Christina, her sister-in-law, had been on her mind.

On Saturday afternoon, Florence knocked on Christina's door. She knew Mark would still be at his saddlery store.

Christina opened the door, looking grim. "I appreciate you coming, Florence." Then her gaze dropped to the baby in Florence's arms and she smiled. "Especially when you bring Iris." Christina put her arms out and Florence handed Iris over.

"Come in."

"Shall I put the tea kettle on for us?" asked Florence since she knew Christina wouldn't be handing Iris back any time soon.

"Sure. That'll give me a chance to play with Iris."

"You can try. She's still too young."

"How did you get here?" asked Christina.

"Carter brought me. He's waiting in the car."

"Oh, tell him to come in."

"No. He's fine. He's using the time to make business calls. Believe me, he'd rather do that than listen to us talk."

"I guess you're right."

Florence walked ahead to the kitchen and as she filled the kettle with water, Christina walked up behind her with Iris in her arms.

"I know why you've come."

Florence turned the water off. "Oh? And why's that?"

"Because of Joy's news."

Florence didn't know what to say. She hadn't wanted to be that obvious. When she had turned on the gas and popped the kettle onto the stovetop, she turned to face Christina. "You're right."

"Well, yes. I did hear Joy's news."

"I knew it would be hard for you to hear."

With one hand, Christina pulled out a chair and sat down. Florence sat opposite. "It's okay, Florence. I've decided to forget about it. Mark said he doesn't mind if we never have *kinner*. I know he's only saying that. He knows how upset I get, so he's doing what he can to make me feel better."

Florence nodded not knowing what to say. It was hard to give her any advice or to truly know what heartache Christina was enduring. Or, to know how Mark truly felt about it.

When Florence just waited, Christina sighed. "People talk about *Gott's* will and His timing. I've waited and waited. Joy didn't have to wait for *Gott's* timing and neither did Honor or Mercy, or anyone else I know. Even you, who left the community, now have a child."

Florence wondered if she shouldn't have visited at all. The last thing she wanted was to make her sister-in-law sad.

"Maybe we should adopt. I don't know. Do you think that's what *Gott* wants us to do?"

"I wouldn't know. I think, though, if He wanted you to do that you'd have an overwhelming desire to do it. Sounds like you don't."

"Nee. I don't and I don't know why. I appreciate you coming here, Florence. I know it's hard. At least I have some baby nieces and nephews to hold."

"How is your sewing business doing?"

"Ach, I have so much work coming my way. That is a blessing because it stops me thinking and feeling

sorry for myself. We were thinking of moving away from here, but we changed our minds about that."

"I'm so glad. I'd miss you and Mark if you moved."

"I figured our problems would just follow us wherever we went." She bent down and kissed the baby on her forehead. "I have to give up and realize it's never going to happen. Let go of it. *Jah,* that's what I'll do." She looked across at Florence and smiled. "I think I feel better already."

CHAPTER 17

AFTER DINNER, the girls were talking behind the house. Cherish found them there after she'd finished the washing up. She was just about to ask why they weren't sitting on the porch when she saw the lit cigarette between Caroline's fingers.

"Oh, you're smoking?" Cherish blurted out.

"*Jah,* she is. I said to come out here because the smoke might go up to Levi and *Mamm's* room."

"My folks don't like me smoking," Caroline said. "Mom used to smoke, so I'm just doing what she did. They can't blame me too much for that." She put the cigarette up to her lips and inhaled.

Cherish coughed when Caroline blew the smoke in her face.

Bliss, who'd been doing the wiping of the dishes,

came around the corner and saw them all standing around. "You're smoking?"

"Yeah."

"It's bad for you."

Caroline raised her eyebrows. "Something's gotta kill you."

"Do your parents let you?"

"Hell no. Mom's always saying, 'do what I say, not what I do.'"

"But if she doesn't smoke now, she should be saying 'don't do what I did,'" Cherish told her.

Caroline frowned. "I'm just sayin' what she says. I'm not a psychiatrist."

Cherish nodded. "Okay." Wanting to get along with the exciting new stranger, Cherish said, "I talked Levi into you staying tonight, and that might become two nights."

"Yeah," said Favor. "Cherish is really good at talking. She can make people do things."

"Thanks, Cherish, that was good of you."

"It's okay. I didn't want you to have to turn around again and go home."

Caroline turned toward Favor and laughed. "I still can't believe you didn't even ask them."

"I couldn't risk them saying no."

"You're so funny. It's something like I'd do.

Although my folks said you could come if you wanted."

"I might get there one day. Maybe."

Caroline took another puff. "I still can't believe I'm here. I've always been fascinated by the Amish ever since you became my pen pal. I can't believe I'm going to one of your meetings tomorrow."

"It's an early start and I know you don't wake up early. I've got a good memory. I remember everything you've written to me."

Caroline let the cigarette slip through her fingers onto the ground below and then she covered it with her foot and squished it into the ground. "I can't see why we have to wake up at six in the morning, though. It's inhumane. I normally don't wake up until—"

Favor finished her sentence. "Eleven. I know."

"Don't you work?" asked Bliss.

"I'm studying from home."

"What are you studying?"

"History, art history."

"Sounds interesting," Cherish said, to be polite.

"Not really. But if I don't study or get a job, my father said he'll cut off my allowance. Studying is pretty easy. I don't even have to travel or get out of bed. I just put my laptop on a couple of pillows and presto, I've got a desk." She giggled.

"Your family must be rich," Bliss said. "We all have to work for money because it goes into the family account."

Caroline's blue eyes opened wide. "You don't get to keep your own money?"

"There's no need to go into all of that," Favor said. "It's just a thing that Levi does. I'm sure many families do it."

"Oh, you must be so poor. I never thought it since you have an orchard. I'll have to pay for my own food while I'm here. You'd have enough to eat, I'm guessing because of the apples."

"We're not poor," said Bliss, "And please don't mention paying for food while you're here. My father is just making sure that he's doing wise things with his money."

Cherish was annoyed. It wasn't *his* money, it was *their* money, but he acted like it was his. Cherish was glad she held back her waitressing tips. She had to have some money that was her own. What Levi didn't know, he couldn't complain about. "Why are you looking forward to our meeting, Caroline?"

"Because I'm gonna record it and put it online. I've already told all my friends I'm coming here.

They're interested to see what my stay here will be like. I might write a book about it one day."

Bliss gulped. "A book about us?"

"No. Not you, and not any of you. It'll be about me, and my stay here."

"Oh. I like Bliss's idea better," said Cherish. "It won't be a good idea to record it. Didn't Favor tell you that we don't like to be photographed? That includes movies and film, which is what you meant when you said record, isn't it?"

"Some Amish don't mind. I've seen them on TV before. Anyway, no one will know I'm doing it. They'll never know. If they never use technology they won't see themselves on the internet."

"Yeah, but we know because you just told us and I'm saying … I'm asking you not to do it. If my step-father finds out he'll make you go home," Favor said.

"Oh, that wouldn't be very good."

"It wouldn't, because I love having you here. We've become such good friends over the years."

"That's right, such good friends. Okay, I won't do it. One thing I've noticed, and I haven't been here very long, is that you have so many rules and every-thing that you must follow. Do this and don't do that. It just seems exhausting."

"We don't have that many rules," Favor commented. "It's all pretty much common sense."

"I don't have any rules where I come from, except the one about me having to study or work. My father won't let me just do nothing. My mother wouldn't care, though. She does whatever she wants and dad doesn't complain. She goes out spending money and hides everything she buys from my father."

"How could she hide things from him?" asked Cherish.

"Easy."

Favor said, "What things does she buy?"

"Jewelry, shoes, bags, and anything else she wants. She puts them at the back of the closet and if he comments when she wears them, she'll tell him she's had them for years." Caroline looked at the girls' feet. "I guess you girls only have three or four pairs of shoes each? Do you wear those black lace up shoes all the time?"

"We do, shoes or boots. I've got some walking shoes apart from these for when I do a lot of walking around the orchard helping Levi do things," said Cherish.

"I didn't come here to talk about shoes, but I do find it interesting. I'm just so excited. Thanks for inviting me here, Favor. And it was nice of your father to let me stay."

"He's not our father," said Cherish. "He's Bliss's father and our stepfather."

"Same thing," Caroline said.

It wasn't the same thing at all, but Cherish wasn't going to say more in front of Bliss because she didn't want to hurt her feelings.

"I remember you writing to me when your father died, Favor. Not yours Bliss, but the other girls' dad."

"I know. I have that day very clear in my head," said Favor. "It was two days after he died and the day before his funeral. You were the first of my pen pals I told. I could barely stop crying long enough to write the words." Favor sniffled and Hope put her arm around her shoulders.

"It was a sad letter. I could tell how much you loved him. He must've been such a nice man."

"He was," all the girls said. Even Bliss said it, because she was old enough to remember Mr. Baker with his ready smile and kind eyes.

The girls talked outside for another half hour before Wilma came out looking for them. She sniffed the air. "I smell smoke. Does anyone else?"

"*Nee.*"

"Must be a fire somewhere. I hope it's not a *haus* or a barn fire. We all must get some sleep now. We have an early start tomorrow," Wilma said.

Caroline stayed in Favor's room as they'd arranged, and they talked halfway into the night.

CHAPTER 18

SUNDAY MORNINGS in the Baker household were the only mornings they didn't have a cooked breakfast. When Caroline walked into the kitchen with Favor, Wilma took the opportunity to explain a few things to their guest. "It's only a simple breakfast on Sunday. It's our day of rest. Because we do no work on Sunday, it includes putting minimal effort into cooking."

"Yeah, Mrs. Bruner, I know that from Favor's letters," Caroline said.

When they sat down, Favor shook some cereal into two bowls.

"I don't usually eat breakfast."

"Are you sure?"

"I'll give it a miss." She leaned over and whispered. "I just have a ciggy and a coffee when I wake up."

Favor looked over at her mother hoping she didn't hear their guest. She was at the sink doing something and didn't flinch. Hopefully, she hadn't heard. "We do have a meal after the meeting's over anyway."

"I'll last just fine until then. I'm excited to know things I haven't learned in your letters. When will I meet Joy and Isaac?"

"I'll just finish this and then I'll take you to meet them. We'll have a few minutes before we need to leave."

"Great."

Favor finished her cereal in double quick time. Then the two walked over to the caravan not far from the house, where Joy and Isaac lived.

"Oh, it's a trailer, camper van thingy."

"Kind of. We call it a caravan."

"You can call it what you like. There's no way to drive it. They must be poor to be living like ..."

Joy stepped out followed by Isaac. Favor hoped they hadn't overheard Caroline, and then Favor introduced the three of them.

"I didn't know you were coming, Caroline. Seems I'm the last to know."

"Same here," said Isaac. "Joy's the second last, I'm the last."

"Favor has told me everything about the both of you. You're the half-sister, right? And, Isaac, you're the illegitimate child?"

Favor froze, not believing her ears. Caroline had the wrong people, and Joy would be so upset that she'd revealed family secrets that were … secret.

"No. This is Joy, my sister, and this is her husband, Isaac. You're thinking about some different people."

"Time's getting away from us. Are you both traveling with us today?" Isaac asked.

Favor grabbed hold of Caroline's arm. "No, we're not. We're going with Hope."

"That's right. You're the one who's got the bun in the oven? No one thought you'd ever get married. Is this the one?" Caroline asked Favor.

Favor didn't know how to answer, and Joy was looking cross with her.

"Whoever thought that about Joy, they didn't know I wanted to marry her," Isaac said, grinning.

"Yes, but you would've had no competition for her, am I right?" asked Caroline.

"Not really," said Joy, letting a little irritation show.

"I'm sure I did, but Joy was nice enough to allow me to think I was the only one," Isaac said.

Favor didn't know what to do. Clearly, Caroline couldn't keep her mouth closed about anything. "We need to go."

"Oh, 'not really' that means yes, or that you don't want to talk about it."

Favor leaned forward and whispered, "I don't think too many of us like answering personal questions."

"Oh, I'm sorry. I'll keep quiet then. I was just trying to make conversation."

"That's good. It's good to make conversation." Favor smiled at Joy and Isaac who didn't look too pleased.

"I get it, though, and I don't want to make people uncomfortable. I've never seen anyone living in a gypsy caravan before."

"Let's go." Favor grabbed Caroline's arm and started walking.

Once they were a few steps away, Caroline pulled her arm back. "No need to be like that."

"Why would you reveal that I told you personal things about them?"

"If they were that personal, you shouldn't have told me, should you?"

Favor was quiet as they both kept walking. Caroline was right. She shouldn't have told her about other people's personal information. The problem was, she had to write about something and her life was so downright boring.

ON THE WAY to the meeting, Cherish and Bliss traveled in the buggy with Levi and Wilma. Hope took Favor and Caroline in a second buggy, and Isaac and Joy went in their own.

"I'm going to ask around today if I can, see if anyone might be interested in buying."

Cherish didn't ask, but she knew Levi was talking about selling the orchard. That was something she would not allow to happen.

She had one ear on what Bliss was talking about and one ear on what Levi was saying.

"I don't know if there'd be anyone in the community who would be interested in buying it," Wilma said.

"Maybe not, but if word gets out that I'm selling

it, it might lead to the right person if *Gott* puts wings on my words."

Wilma giggled. "'Wings on your words,' to carry them to the right buyer so he can hear about it?"

"Exactly."

When Wilma and Levi chuckled at the same time, it didn't exactly please Cherish to see her mother and stepfather were getting along. That was only because Wilma was now going along with everything Levi said. That kept him happy. Or maybe *Mamm* saw his good side because, as she had found out for herself, Levi wasn't all bad—not all the time.

"Are you listening to anything I'm saying, Cherish?" Bliss asked.

"*Jah,* every word of it."

Bliss moved closer to Cherish. "Well, what did I just say?"

"You said that ... you were talking about your rabbits and how you're keeping them until you find a good home."

"That's right."

Cherish smiled to herself. It wasn't hard to guess that. That's what she was always talking about.

Obviously Wilma had overheard. "I agreed that you can keep ONE rabbit, Bliss. All the rest will have to go."

"And I'm trying, really I am."

"Try harder," Levi said. "Or I'll take them and give them away myself."

"I will, I will."

When Cherish saw Bliss's bottom lip started to wobble, she almost felt sorry for her. She leaned over and patted her shoulder. "It's fine. It'll be okay."

Bliss said. "I can't just give my rabbits to anybody. I have to make sure they go to a good home. Adam understands that."

"That's why you should make sure your rabbit can't reproduce any more. I'll give you the money to have the animal neutered, Bliss," Levi said.

"You will?"

"Yes, we can arrange to have that done next week."

"Denke, Dat. That would be *wunderbaar."*

"I'll take it out of your cafe money," Levi added.

"I'll see if we can put up a notice in the window at the café about the rabbits for sale. And then when you're working, you can interview anyone who's interested in taking one of your rabbits," Cherish said.

"Make sure you tell him it's not for eating," Wilma said. "But … how would you know if they don't tell you?"

Cherish was shocked at her mother. Didn't she know how sensitive Bliss was about the rabbit? *"Mamm,* don't say that to her."

Wilma giggled, but she was the only one who was doing so. Even Levi wasn't laughing.

CHAPTER 19

WHEN THE MEETING was well underway, Caroline pulled her cell phone from her jeans pocket. Then she tapped something on the screen and held it up.

Cherish, who was sitting on one side of Favor, dug Favor in the ribs. "She's recording on her phone."

Favor put up her hand and covered Caroline's phone. "Stop that. You know we don't want you to do that."

"Don't be silly. There are lots of things on YouTube like this."

"Yeah, I won't be responsible for it when Levi finds out about it."

Caroline put her phone in her lap. "I don't get this. I thought you didn't like him."

"He's okay."

"That's not what you said in all the letters. Maybe I should say things to him about what you've told me."

"What are you talking about? What kind of things?"

"All the things you wrote in your letter that you said about him, and all the things your sisters have said. You've told me a lot."

Favor was shocked at her friend. "That's before we got to know him. He's not so bad now."

"Still… If you let me film I won't tell."

"Switch it off please."

She put the phone in her lap. "There, happy?"

"Yes I am."

Caroline giggled. "I was only joking. You should've seen your face. I won't tell Levi anything. Of course I wouldn't."

When a man got up to sing, Caroline whispered to Favor, "I should be recording him. He's amazing. He'd get discovered for sure. He could win any talent show. Why don't women sing? You told me once, but I forget."

"They just don't. Not at our meetings, but it's perfectly okay anywhere else, just not in a meeting."

Favor was starting to regret inviting Caroline. It was hard to believe this was the person with whom she'd been exchanging letters.

At the meal after the meeting, Favor saw Cherish and Caroline off to one side looking at Caroline's phone. She sneaked up on them to hear Caroline say, "And look how many hits I've got already, two hundred, and I've only just uploaded it." She looked over Caroline's shoulder to see that she'd filmed the meeting—including the image of her telling Caroline to turn it off.

Favor grabbed the phone from Caroline. "Are you serious? I asked you to turn it off."

"I did." Caroline took her phone back. "And then I turned it on again because I had to upload it. Look how many hits it's got already and it's only been an hour or so. It's gone viral."

"Oh, a virus, that's awful," Cherish said.

"No, not a virus, it's gone viral."

Cherish was totally confused. In her world, a virus was bad. If it was spreading, wasn't that worse? "A viral is good?"

"Yes, and you just say 'viral,' not 'a viral.'"

"Please take it down," Favor said.

"Can you take it off?" Cherish asked. "Or is it stuck there?"

"I could do it, but I don't want to."

"Caroline, please take it off," Favor whined.

"Alright then, to stop you being so upset I'll take it off."

"I'll watch you do it," said Favor just to make sure that it was actually done. Favor saw her press a button that said 'delete.'

"There. It's done. Are you happy now?"

Favor smiled. "Yes."

Cherish frowned. "I've heard once something is uploaded to the internet it's uploaded forever. I heard you couldn't delete it."

"Well I have deleted it. You both just saw me do it, just now."

"Okay," said Cherish. "I'm just saying what I heard. I overhear people at work talk about things like that."

"Then they don't know what they're talking about. Neither do you if you didn't know what viral means."

"Do you want anything more to eat?" Favor asked Caroline.

Caroline patted her tight jeans that covered her

flat stomach. "I've never had so much to eat. It's all good, too. Although I do miss my burgers from back home."

"You've only been here for one day," said Cherish. And, it was one day too long, as far as Cherish was concerned.

"I have a take-out burger nearly every day."

"You can come to the café I work at tomorrow and have one there," Cherish offered.

"Are the burgers good?"

"I think they are, but I don't know if you would think they are."

"It won't hurt to try them. How will I get there?"

Favor said, "We can have Joy drive us. Maybe she could bring all the girls and we'll have a day out."

"That'll be fun."

Cherish noticed that Caroline said the words, but her face didn't reflect what she was saying. Then her face lit up when she saw Fairfax.

"Who is that guy with Hope?" Caroline asked.

"That's her boyfriend, Fairfax. He's joining our community," said Favor.

Cherish added, "He's in the process."

"Very interesting. I would like to talk to him and see why he made that decision."

"Are you thinking of making that decision too?" asked Cherish.

"No, I couldn't do it. There is no way, but I'd like to find out why he did. How long has he been together with Hope?"

"It depends what you mean by *together,*" said Cherish. "It could be about a year or more."

"Where does he live?"

"He's staying on the Millers' dairy farm, and working for them. They're his host family. Whoever wants to join us must stay with a family for a few months. Half a year, mainly, or thereabouts."

"To see if they'll like it?"

"Yes, and if they do, then they take the instructions, which are like lessons, and then get baptized."

"The dairy's not that far from where we live," said Favor.

"If I wanted to talk to him, how would I do that?"

"We'll take you to him right now."

"Oh, I don't want Hope to get the wrong idea."

"The wrong idea about what?" asked Favor.

"I don't want her to think I'm interested in her boyfriend."

"No, she wouldn't think that."

Favor linked her arm with Caroline's and together they headed over to Hope and Fairfax. Just before they reached the couple, Hope walked away leaving Fairfax on his own.

Favor introduced them. Then Favor made sure she hung around while they made small talk. She wasn't one hundred percent certain that she could trust Caroline. Not after the cell phone business.

CHAPTER 20

THAT NIGHT AFTER A LIGHT SUPPER, the girls
went to bed and Cherish was rinsing out her dog's
dish and then she put it back where it always was, by
the back door. When she stepped back into the
kitchen, she saw Levi standing there in the middle of
the kitchen.

"Did I do something wrong?" Everything she'd
done in the past few days whizzed through her mind.

"*Nee.* Let's sit and have a talk." When they were
both sitting at the kitchen table, Levi began, "Cherish, I think out of all the girls you're the most in
tune with the orchard."

"Me?"

"*Jah,* and I know that by little things you've said.
You have a lot of knowledge."

Cherish was pleased to hear it.

"We've had two harvests that weren't much good. This time, I want you to make the call for when we should begin the harvest."

"Really? Me?"

"*Jah.* I'm leaving it up to you to say when we should start the harvest."

Cherish coughed. Then she cleared her throat. Never had she been given such responsibility. but now she was in a dilemma with her old plan to ruin the orchard so it would be hard to sell. *"Denke."*

In that moment, Cherish knew that she couldn't ruin the harvest. She had to do what was right.

She hated that somewhere along the way she had developed a conscience. "I'd say we only have another couple of days."

"You make the call, let me know and I'll get all our pickers here whenever you say."

"Denke, Levi," she said again.

"What for?"

"For trusting me."

"I know you'll do a good job." He held up his finger at her. "Just remember this though. Everyone is relying on you."

She gave a weak smile. His expression let her know he wasn't being horrible. He was genuine about allowing her to do this. He knew he'd messed things up and he wanted to make things right. "I won't let anybody down."

"I know you won't."

"So, it sounds like a lot of work. Should I leave my job?"

Levi chuckled. "You've only been working a few shifts in these last months. Did you sacrifice some work so Bliss could also get a job there at the café?"

"Nee, I didn't. I don't think that's the way it is. They gave Bliss a job when one of the other workers quit, and then the place got quieter all of a sudden."

"I hope that had nothing to do with Bliss."

"Of course not, she's a good worker. Another coffee shop opened up nearby and that hasn't been good for us."

"Maybe you should get a job there if they're busier."

"Nee! I can't work for the opposition."

"When you're working for them, they'll no longer be the competition."

"I didn't think of that, but I'm used to everyone and Rocky's so good to work for. He's really good."

Wilma walked into the kitchen and stopped still. "What is this?"

"We're just talking," Cherish said.

"I've never seen the two of you talk before."

"Time for bed. *Gut nacht.*" Cherish left the room. When she was halfway up the stairs, she heard Levi talking to Wilma.

"Perhaps I will let Caroline stay for a few days. We can't hold onto them too tightly. They'll need to make their own decisions in life. Perhaps having Caroline here wearing her men's clothing and living the life she does, will show our girls that they don't want that life."

"What if it shows them that they do?" asked Wilma.

"We can't protect them forever. Maybe *Gott* sent Caroline here to test them."

"I can see that you could be right especially since Favor arranged it. It was something more like I would've expected of Cherish."

Cherish was upset with her mother for saying such a thing, although she had to admit her mother was right, and then she was even more upset when Levi agreed with *Mamm.*

"I feel much better about her staying here now. You're such a wise man, Levi."

"Do not forsake wisdom and she shall protect you."

Wilma chortled. "I did a good thing when I married you."

"Nee, I did. Whoever finds a *fraa* findeth a *gut* thing."

Wilma laughed, and then Levi laughed.

Levi's laughter was a sound that Cherish had never heard before. And, what *Mamm* said wasn't even funny. Cherish walked up the rest of the stairs and went into her room and started her nightly routine. She was in the middle of brushing out her hair before she changed into her nightgown, when a thought occurred to her.

Levi was in a good mood right now and it would be a long time before another good mood happened. She had to get everything now while the getting was good. She placed her prayer *kapp* back on her head, pushed up all her hair into it, and then headed downstairs. By this time, Wilma and Levi had moved from the kitchen and were sitting in the living room.

"Levi, I have something to ask you."

Wilma looked up from her knitting and snapped, "Now is not a good time. Can't you see he's reading The Bulletin?"

Levi folded the Amish newspaper in two and placed it down on the table in front of him. "It's okay, Wilma. What is it, Cherish?" He took off his reading glasses and held them in his hand.

She moved and sat down on the rug in front of him. "For many years, before you took over the orchard, we had the *Englisch* school children come in right before the harvest and we'd take them on a tour. We'd show them how the orchard operates and let them taste all our varieties of apples, and we used to make them bags that they could take home with them and the teachers would come with them and we'd show them all around the orchard telling them about everything. They really enjoyed it. And it's a good way to be involved in the community. Not just our Amish community but the overall community, the broader community."

"That might be a good idea, Cherish."

"Do you really think so? The girls will all help. I'll get some of my friends to help too."

"*Jah.* I think it might be a good thing. What money will it bring in?"

"None, but we are doing our part for the community."

"Let them, Levi," *Mamm* said. "The girls used to have such fun making up the gift bags. They have so little fun these days. It'll be good for them."

Cherish smiled at her mother for the unexpected

help.

"Hmm. Sounds like it's going to cost us."

"Not much, though. It's worth it," said Cherish. "When you see all the smiling faces of the children. Sometimes one or two of them bring their parents to buy apples and other products."

"And who is going to be in charge of arranging all this?"

"I could be."

"I don't know if you should be in charge of it since you're in charge of that other thing we talked about."

"I can do it all. And, what I can't do, I'll hand over the responsibility to one of the other girls. It would be good for my organizational skills. One day, I'll need to run my own household, and perhaps a farm."

Then Wilma threw in a negative comment, making Cherish wish she hadn't mentioned the word 'farm.' "What if you decide you need to visit your farm to check on your man who's looking after it?"

"I won't need to go for a while. Not until after the harvest. And the children only come right before the harvest or at the start, so they're not in the way of the actual harvest with all the workers."

"They wouldn't get in the way," said Wilma. "But

they could take us away from harvest work."

Cherish smiled again at her mother, wishing she would just keep quiet.

"You can contact the schools, can't you, Cherish? You know which ones usually came out?" Wilma asked.

"I do. I can make all the arrangements because I used to listen to what Florence did." When she saw Levi was still not convinced, she added, "And it would be good for Bliss to be involved to have fun talking to the children and teaching them things."

"*Jah*, Bliss did want to be a teacher. She mentioned it once or twice."

"And she might be considered for that soon. With so many children being born in the community, they'll need more teachers before too long."

"Well there you go—that might be a very good way for her to do something like that."

"I like the idea, Levi, don't you?" Wilma asked.

"I'm thinking about it."

"I will just get in touch with the schools, all the schools who used to do it."

"I'm sure they would love to bring the students along again."

Levi looked at Wilma. "You think it's a good idea?"

"Jah. If the girls want to do it, it might be a good thing. And the girls did enjoy it, making up the gift bags for the children."

"You said that already, *Mamm."* Cherish spoke nicely so it didn't sound like she was growing impatient with her mother.

Levi frowned and stared at Cherish. "What's involved in these gift bags?"

"Oh just things like toffee apples and some apple seeds. Nothing that costs anything really."

"As long as it doesn't cost very much I don't see that there would be a problem with it."

"Denke, Levi. All the girls will look forward to that this year. And it'll be happening very soon. Since it's nearly harvest time again, I'll get on the phone first thing tomorrow and start arranging things."

"I like the way you think, Cherish. You have a good mind."

"You think I do?"

Levi grinned. *"Jah,* I'm not making up stories. I feel good about it," he said. "I can see your *mudder* is keen for this to go ahead and if it makes the children happy then we'll do it."

"Denke, Levi. I can't wait. I've missed them coming here these last couple of years."

CHAPTER 21

THE NEXT MORNING, Cherish ran to the barn and grabbed the small notebook with all the numbers written down. There were three schools that used to bring their children out. She thumbed through until she found the numbers of each. Then she waited until after nine and made the calls.

Every school she called, she got the same answer. They'd already booked all their excursions for the year. Two of the schools went on to explain that the parents of their students would complain if they tried to fit in another. Cherish told them they'd be interested in having the children next year.

Now Cherish was let down. She had so much knowledge to pass on with no one to listen to her. Then she thought of Caroline. She'd teach her. Surely she'd be interested in finding out more about their beautiful apple trees and how the harvesting worked. And, for sure she'd be fascinated by the cider making process.

After that, they could put her to work making jams and chutneys from the early fruit that had fallen. That's what Wilma had planned for the day.

As soon as Favor and Caroline were at the breakfast table, Cherish volunteered to make the breakfast. Hope had gone to work, and Bliss had gone out with Wilma and Levi to get some new shoes.

"What will we do today?" Caroline asked Favor.

"I'm glad you asked that," said Cherish, "because I thought we could spend the day in the orchard. I'll show you everything and how to make the cider. Then in the afternoon, our mother is coming back to make some jams and pickles."

"Thanks for the offer, but I was hoping we'd go out somewhere. Maybe go into town."

"You can do that any old time. How often do you get to stay at a place like this?"

"This is the first."

"Make use of it then. Didn't you say something about writing a book one day? It'll be a pretty boring book if it's all about you going into town to find boys."

Caroline opened her mouth in shock and then laughed. "You're funny, Cherish."

"Cherish, I really don't think Caroline wants to know how to pick an apple off a tree or how to store apples, or why the fruit from different places on the tree are different colors."

When Caroline giggled, Cherish knew there was no hope. She finished making the breakfast of bacon, eggs and toast. After breakfast was done, she watched Caroline and Favor move outside with their cups full of coffee.

Then they were behind the house. Cherish could see them clearly from the kitchen window. Caroline placed her cup on the ground while she lit up a cigarette.

Cherish washed the dishes. Then she walked in the orchard on her own. Looking at the fruit, she knew it was time. As soon as Levi got home, she'd tell him.

IT WAS JUST before lunchtime that Levi got home. Bliss had a new pair of shoes and Wilma had something as well that she was carrying in a brown paper bag. Cherish ran up to Levi as he was unhitching the buggy.

"We should harvest tomorrow."

He looked up. "Are you sure?"

"Positive. Come with me and I'll show you the signs."

"Nee. If you say it, I'll believe it."

"It won't take a moment."

"Nee. I have people to call to make arrangements for tomorrow. We'll have a big day." He rubbed his chin. "Does your *mudder* know? She'll have to arrange the food for everyone."

"I told you first."

"Tell her now, and I'll make the calls as soon as I tend to the horse." He patted the bay horse on his shoulder.

Cherish turned around and walked back to the house. Levi was confusing. He and her mother had made a long trip to visit someone near where her older sisters lived to learn about running an orchard. Now, he couldn't be bothered to look at the signs. "Can I have the day off tomorrow to stay here? I'm supposed to go to work."

"Don't they need you?"

"No. They'll have enough time to find someone else to cover my shift."

"*Denke*. That would be good to have you here."

"I'll tell *Mamm* about the harvest starting officially tomorrow and then I'll call my boss."

Levi gave her a nod.

Cherish left him, and walked into the house. No sooner had she told her mother than a car pulled up. Cherish looked out the window to see a man getting out of his car. Levi was nowhere about.

"*Mamm,* who's that?"

They both looked out the living room window. "It's Eric Brosley."

"Wasn't that one of *Dat's* friends?"

"As much as you can call an *Englisher* a friend, *jah*. He was one of his apple-growing friends."

"That's right. He's the one helping Florence with her orchard."

"*Jah,* helping our competition. He's no friend of mine any longer."

Cherish knew that Florence's orchard wasn't competition. No local orchards were in competition with each other. There was enough business for everyone, but there was no use saying that to her mother. Sometimes *Mamm* just seemed to need something to complain about.

"What's he doing here?" Wilma asked.

"We'll soon find out. He's coming to the door."

"Leave this to me." Wilma bustled past Cherish and opened the front door.

"Hello, Wilma. How are you doing?"

"Fine," Cherish heard her mother respond, curtly.

"I'm here to talk to your husband if I might?"

"His name's Levi."

"Yes, Levi Bruner. I'm here to talk with him. Well, with both of you if I may."

"What's it about?" *Mamm* asked.

"It's about the orchard."

"I expected it might be. Take a seat in the living room." Wilma showed Eric into the living room and he sat down next to Cherish, who'd quickly sat down.

"Hello," Cherish greeted him.

Wilma said to Cherish, "Could you find Levi?"

"Sure." Cherish rose to her feet. As soon as she was at the door, Levi appeared. "There you are. There's a man here to see you. Eric Brosley."

Levi nodded. *"Denke."*

He walked past her, and then Cherish made herself scarce, taking herself to the kitchen where she could hear what was going on.

"I don't believe we've ever met," she heard Levi say after Wilma introduced them.

"I'll come right to the point. I have someone who's asked me to inquire whether you'd be selling the orchard. They heard on the grapevine you're willing to sell."

"For the right price everything's for sale. Nearly everything. Why doesn't this man approach me himself?"

"He will, but he's asked me to make the initial inquiries."

Then Wilma said, "We need to know who it is before we know if we want to sell. Or how much we want to sell for."

"Are you saying the orchard will be different prices for different people?"

"Yes, that's right," Wilma said.

"We'll have to talk about that between ourselves," Levi told Eric, meaning he didn't entirely agree with Wilma.

It was obvious that Wilma thought the interested potential buyer was Florence, but what if it was someone else? That meant Florence had competition for the orchard.

"I won't keep you. Here's my business card. It's got all my numbers on it. If you ever do decide you want to sell please give me a call."

"Will do, and thank you for stopping by," Levi said.

"I'll show you out."

Cherish heard her mother's footsteps travel across the floor to the door. Then she heard the door close and the footsteps sounded again, back to the couch.

"You know who's interested, don't you?" Wilma asked.

"Who?"

"Florence and Carter. Either of them or both."

"*Nee,* I don't think so. Florence wrote me a letter. It's someone else."

"*Nee.* It's one of them. Eric has designed their new orchard from the drainage system to the buying of the plants. They are in thick with him."

"Still, if it is two buyers that could drive up our price."

Now Cherish was mad with herself for telling Levi to start the harvest the next day. She should've just let the fruit rot on the trees if that would help Florence get her orchard back. In Cherish's mind, it was rightfully Florence's.

CHAPTER 22

"Is this what you usually do after dinner?" Caroline asked.

"Mostly," said Wilma with a smile. "It's relaxing and keeps us busy."

"Mostly we have a Bible study first," said Cherish. "But Levi's tired tonight and we've got a big day tomorrow, so we're just sewing and knitting."

"What do you do after dinner when you're at home, Caroline?" asked Cherish.

"Go out with my friends, go to a restaurant or bar. If I'm staying home I'm having pizza in front of a movie."

"You don't do anything with your hands?" asked Wilma.

"Only video games when I'm holding the controller." Caroline laughed.

Or smoking, Cherish thought.

"Video games. Well that sounds quite interesting."

Favor was pleased her mother was trying to get along with Caroline. "And the other thing she does with her hands is write me letters."

"Yeah. Favor is the only one I write letters to. I email all my other friends, or text them."

Favor was pleased to be counted as a friend and not just a pen pal. She had so few friends. She didn't need many when she had so many sisters.

"How long is it that you two have been writing to one another?" asked Wilma.

"Many years. I think it's eight."

"Remember, *Mamm,* when our school had a program where we wrote to people from other schools?"

"Somehow I ended up with Favor's name and address. Oh, Mrs. Bruner, what you're doing looks lovely. Is that knitting?"

Wilma giggled. "Of course this is knitting. Don't you know what knitting is?"

"I thought it was. How would I start doing some?"

"Sit here by me, and I'll cast on some stitches for you. I've got a spare pair of needles. You can knit a square for practice."

Caroline sat beside her and soon she had a few inches of plain and purl. "I like this. It's so peaceful sitting here with no noise except us talking and we're all making things and not wasting time."

"I'm glad you're enjoying yourself." Wilma smiled.

"I'll make us some hot tea before bed," Hope said, as she stood up.

"I'll help." Caroline crisscrossed her needles over and Wilma stopped her.

"No. You always finish the row before you walk away. You'll loosen your knitting and it wouldn't be even. And, you have such lovely even stitches."

"Okay, I'll finish the row. Thanks for letting me know." When she finished the row, she joined Hope in the kitchen.

"I'm just waiting on the kettle to boil." Hope proceeded to pull out cups and saucers from the cupboard.

"What shall I do?" Caroline asked.

"It's all done, but you can talk to me."

Caroline put her hands on her hips. "Fairfax is so nice. Where did you meet him?"

"Believe it or not, he's lived on the next-door property all my life and I only just met him recently."

"I can see how that would happen. The orchard is so large. I've walked around it and never got to the back of it. It went on forever, and with him not being in the community, you would have had no chance to meet."

"My father met them. Fairfax's mother told me that. Fairfax's parents have moved now, to Florida. They've retired."

"I know. Fairfax told me."

Hope's eyes opened wide. "You talked to Fairfax?"

"Yeah, at the meeting the other day. He really is nice and so handsome."

"I know."

"So you have a boyfriend and Bliss has one. No one else?"

"Bliss is a little young to have a boyfriend. Adam, well, he's just a friend, really."

"Ah, I see what's going on. Bliss has a pretend boyfriend."

Hope smiled. "Kind of."

"I'll remember that. What's his name?"

"His name's Adam Wengerd. They bonded over rabbits. It's a long story."

"So her boyfriend is Adam. I remember the story now. Favor told me all about it in her letters. She tells me everything. Not just about her, but about all of you. I know everything about everyone." She leaned forward and whispered, "Sometimes she writes so much I need to skip over it. I'd still be reading them now if I read everything."

Hope giggled. "I don't know how she does it. She must have about twenty pen pals."

"She'd have to spend every spare moment writing."

"She does."

The kettle boiling interrupted them. Hope poured the boiled water into the tea pot and then they placed it onto the tray to carry out to the living room.

CHAPTER 23

WHILE EVERYONE WAS busy at home with the harvest, Bliss had been called into work thanks to Cherish taking the day off. Bliss didn't like to say no in case she lost her job over it. When she was finished with her workday, she walked out looking for Adam who was supposed to be collecting her. His buggy was there, but when she looked inside, he wasn't.

Then she spotted a couple up the street and realized the man was Adam. The woman was Caroline. Bliss wasn't happy that they were laughing and seemed to be enjoying each other's company.

Caroline was obviously a flirt. She'd been interested in Fairfax, couldn't stop talking about him, and now she was talking with Adam. Bliss walked over trying to calm her temper that was bubbling under the surface.

Adam straightened up when he saw her and the smile was immediately gone. He looked like he'd been caught out. "There you are, Bliss. Sorry, I didn't notice the time slipping away."

Bliss couldn't help glaring at Caroline. Adam was hers, and Caroline knew it.

"Hi, Bliss." Caroline smiled at her and then looked at Adam. "Can I grab a ride?"

"We aren't going home," Bliss said.

"Where are you going?"

Bliss looked at Adam hoping he'd say something to save the situation. It was the least he could do after enjoying another woman's company.

"We can take you home, Caroline." He looked at Bliss. "Then we'll go on our own from there, Bliss, *jah?*"

"Okay." Bliss nodded, half satisfied about his response. There was no easy answer for him. He'd appear rude if he left Caroline there after she'd asked for a ride and taking her home was a nice thing to do.

"I'll sit in the back," Caroline announced.

There was never any doubt about that, Bliss thought.

Once they were on the road, Caroline leaned over between the two of them.

"I didn't realize you two were an item. It was a surprise."

"We are," answered Bliss abruptly.

"You just don't *look* like a couple."

Adam chuckled, tossing his brown hair back until the sun lit up the golden streaks. "Why's that?"

"A couple?" asked Bliss before Caroline could answer Adam.

"Yeah, like boyfriend and girlfriend."

"We are," Bliss said again, turning around to look at her.

Caroline sat back and was quiet for a few moments. Then she said, "If I knew you two were involved with one another I never would've asked for a ride home. You must think I'm horribly rude."

"No we don't," said Adam, earning a sideways glance from Bliss.

"I still can't get used to the zero-technology thing you Amish have got going on. I mean, I knew it would be like this, but still .... At least I've got my cell phone, but most of the time there's no reception. And talk about chores, Wilma insists you girls keep cleaning the house. It can't get any cleaner than clean. Then it gets so dark so early and there's really nothing to do but sleep unless you like to sew, or play boring games, which I don't."

"And, you're here because you're Favor's pen pal?" asked Adam.

"That's right."

"Why aren't you with Favor?" asked Bliss. "I was told you were here to help with the harvest and the harvest started today."

"I don't know. I was told nothing about the harvest. There's something going on between her and her folks. I know they don't like me. They won't let her go anywhere with me. Anyway, why aren't you helping with the harvest, Bliss?"

"I will be for the next few days. It'll be work from dawn until dusk. There's so much to do. *Dat* said I could work today, spend some time with Adam and then start tomorrow."

"Yeah, well, just as well you Amish have so many children. You can spread out the work load."

Adam stopped at the bottom of the drive of the Baker orchard. "Can I let you out here? It's a little bit crowded in the driveway."

"Sure." Caroline jumped out. "Thanks for the ride. I'll see you both later."

As soon as she was out, Bliss whispered, "Quick, let's go."

Adam laughed. "Okay. Look, you've got no need to worry about her."

"Worry about who?"

He smiled at her. "No one. I'm thinking of making the move here permanently."

"What? Are you doing this because of her?"

"I'm doing it because of you. What other reason would I have to stay around these parts when I could go home?"

"That makes me very happy."

"That's the idea. Eventually, I want to make you happy every day. One day, we can keep rabbits together."

"Yeah, but not too many."

"Just a couple. I'm done with the breeding of the rabbits. It's too hard to find good homes."

"I don't blame you for getting upset about my rabbit getting out. It must have upset you and been a shock for you."

"It was, but it turned out well."

She saw him turn down a side road. "Where are we going?"

"It's a surprise."

"A surprise for me?"

"Yes."

She had no idea what it could possibly be when

she saw large, industrial sheds. Then he directed the horse and buggy off the road and into a parking lot. "Let's go. I've got something to show you." He stopped the buggy and ran around to her side and waited for her to get out. He took hold of her hand, walked over to the building, and pulled up a roller door. She saw a large enclosure standing within the shed.

"Oh, I love this. This would be a perfect outdoor pen for my rabbit."

"That's what it's meant to be. A livestock enclosure."

"This is my surprise?"

"Yes, and not only that, I've just gone in as partner with Andrew Weeks now, and we're opening a business together. We've already got clients, and orders waiting."

Bliss smiled, but behind that smile she wondered if he was moving here for the business he was starting with Andrew, or was he moving here for her?

He stepped forward and put his arm around her. "Are you pleased?"

"I'm so happy. Probably the happiest I've ever been."

He kissed her on her forehead. "I'm hoping this

will make us a good living for a good life. There are people crying out for things like this."

"Outside animal enclosures?"

"Yes, and similar things that are custom-made."

He showed her around the rest of the building. As well as the massive working area, there was a small kitchen and small bathroom.

As they were walking back to the buggy, she said, "How did you get the idea to start this business with Andrew?"

"We've been talking about it for a while. We had the idea when I was here the first time. We met at the mud sale where I met you."

Bliss's mind traveled back to the mud sale where Cherish spotted him and claimed him as her own. She had made sure Cherish was over him before she wrote to him after he left. Pretty soon he came back. It pleased her that he was a man of action. A man who would do things instead of procrastinating over them.

When Adam climbed up into the buggy after her, he looked over at her. "Why are you smiling?"

"I'm happy for you, happy for us."

"Good. That makes it all worth it, moving forward, putting all the hard work into things."

"When do you get started?"

"We have to fit this place out with everything and I think we can start work early next week. You and I can still see each other every day, but it might mean that we see each other a little less each day."

"That'll be fine. I don't mind. You can come for dinner most nights. We've always got plenty and then you won't have to worry about getting yourself anything to eat. It'll save you a lot of time."

"I like the sound of that. Andrew and I are thinking of renting a house together."

Bliss wasn't sure if she was happy with that. Two single men together. What if they talked about girls? What if Andrew didn't think she was good enough for Adam?

"What do you think about that?" he asked.

"I think it's a *wunderbaar* idea. Have you had a look at any places?"

"I'm meeting him to look at one at six this evening. Every spare moment, I'll come and help with your harvest."

"That'll make *Dat* pleased. We always need many hands at harvest time." Bliss wasn't happy about the housing idea but she wasn't going to let him know it. She didn't want him to think she was the kind of girl who would complain about everything he did.

"Don't get me wrong, Bliss. Everything I'm doing

from now on is for both of us. I'm determined to make us a future together."

Bliss smiled at him and she was happy, but he never mentioned when they would marry. Even though she was a little too young, she wanted to get reassurance—a firm date or timeframe. Was he thinking of marrying in two years, five years or perhaps ten? Because if it was going to be ten years away, she wouldn't be happy with that. She wanted it to be two years. She couldn't wait to marry Adam.

CHERISH WAS EXHAUSTED after the first day of harvest, still she had a little energy left before lights out to write a letter to Malachi. She hadn't heard from him in a while. She'd asked him to write once a week to keep her updated about what was going on with her farm.

CHAPTER 24

"*Denke*, Levi. That's very generous. That's why I married you."

Cherish heard Wilma talking to Levi just before she stepped into the kitchen. It was too late to about-face and walk out. They'd both seen her. She had to keep walking in. "What's generous?"

Wilma looked up at her from the kitchen table where she sat with Levi. "Levi has offered Joy and Isaac to stay in one of his rental houses for no rent."

"Oh, you have rental houses, Levi?" She'd heard that he did, but he'd never mentioned that to any of them.

"I do."

"Can I stay in one of them too? I can even pay a little out of my pay check."

Levi laughed, but Wilma didn't.

"What's so funny?" Cherish asked.

"You're too young to live alone," her mother said. "Why must you constantly wear me out?"

"I don't feel too young. So, can I if Bliss was to live there too?" Surely he wouldn't charge his own daughter rent.

Wilma explained, *"Nee.* Your sister and Isaac will not be staying there totally for free and neither *should* they get such a hand out. Young people have to know that what they want requires work. Isaac will be doing repairs to the *haus,* in return for the free rent."

"So there's a catch and it's really not free at all?"

"Cherish—"

"I know, go to my room." Cherish's shoulders drooped.

"Jah, and you're grounded for a week," Wilma added. "Except when you have to go to work."

"Okay, suits me. I don't really go anywhere anyway. I just stay here and slave away wearing my fingers to the bone, chipping all my fingernails to the quick, causing them to bleed."

Wilma held her head in her hands. "Just go!"

Cherish felt bad when she saw how upset *Mamm* was. "I'm sorry. I didn't mean it like that. Okay? I was just trying to understand what 'free' meant. In my mind it's not free if other obligations need to be met. On my farm, Malachi isn't staying for free because he's doing work so it's—"

"You asked and your *mudder* has answered," said Levi. "It's none of your concern, anyway. It's between me and Isaac."

"I'm going." Cherish turned around, left the kitchen, and then walked up the stairs to her bedroom. She wasn't trying to argue. She was only trying to understand the situation. Wasn't she a part of the family? It didn't feel like it sometimes with Levi around.

Grounded for one week?

Surely *Mamm* would forget what she said.

She normally did.

THAT NIGHT CHERISH walked past Favor's open bedroom door and saw Favor lying on a mattress on the floor. She stuck her head in and saw that Caroline was nowhere to be seen. "Why aren't you in the bed?"

"Caroline was sleeping on the mattress and that

was fine for the first couple of nights, but now she made me give her my bed."

"Firstly, she's the guest, so shouldn't you have offered your bed?"

"Nee. I love my bed. Would you give up your bed?"

"I would. Where is she?"

"In the bathroom." Favor whispered, "It's not only the bed, she talks non-stop way into the night."

"About what?"

"I don't know … everything. All the little details of her life and everything she's planning. She just goes on, and on, and on."

"What do you tell her?"

"Nothing really. I don't get a chance. Just about what I've done that day, if she wasn't with me."

"Mamm would say, you were the one who invited her."

"I'm not complaining. Okay, I guess I am." Favor laughed. "I shouldn't complain, should I?"

"Nee." Cherish kneeled down beside her.

"I do love having her here, but I get so annoyed when she talks about Adam."

"How much does she talk about him?"

"Just here and there through the day. She asks me things like where Bliss went and what they did."

"Does she ask how serious their relationship is?"

"Nee. But I told her to forget him."

"Good. That's good to hear."

"You think the same thing I'm thinking."

"What?" asked Cherish with her eyebrows scrunched in confusion.

"She likes Adam. That's what." Favor put her head in her hands and cried.

"Cut it out. Why are you so upset? He's not your boyfriend." Cherish pulled Favor's hands away from her face.

"Because Bliss will be upset, and then she'll blame me for bringing Caroline here. I get the blame for everything."

"Oh, now you're saying you get the blame? I'm the one who gets the blame. You're the one who thinks she's invisible."

"Jah, that too. The only time I'm not invisible is when I'm getting the blame."

"I doubt Adam would like Caroline. Is she a rabbit lover?"

"Nee, but she could pretend to be one."

Cherish swiped a hand through the air. "You don't need to worry about her. Adam's only interested in Bliss, believe me. They're inseparable."

"Hmm. I'm not so sure about that."

"It's true. I did everything I could to make him like me and I couldn't. Besides that, Caroline's an *Englisher*."

"Florence left for Carter. Adam could leave if he's in love with someone."

"He doesn't need to because he's in love with Bliss, silly."

Favor smiled. "Do you think so?"

"*Jah*. Everyone knows it … Caroline is pretty, though."

"I know. Why did you have to say that, Cherish? That's what I'm worried about."

Cherish giggled. "If he's swayed by a pretty face, Bliss would be better off without him."

"Easy to say, not so easy for Bliss to think about or to live with."

"I know what you mean. Most things in life are that way, I've found out."

Then, Caroline came back into the room and side-stepped around Cherish to get to the bed. Before she sat, she saw Favor's face. "Why are you upset?"

"I'm not. I just had something in my eye."

Cherish had to change the subject. "We're having a lovely family dinner tomorrow night. We did ask Christina and Mark, but they couldn't come."

"I met them on Sunday," Caroline said.

"Then we've got Ada and Samuel, that's our mother and Levi's best friends, and then Fairfax is coming too. Our mother wanted Fairfax to come for some reason. I think to ask him about his parents."

"Yes," Favor added. "She's fixated on getting to know her future son-in-laws' families at the moment."

"So, is Adam coming too?"

Favor stared at Cherish. "Is he, Cherish?"

"I'm not certain. Maybe." Cherish hoped that Favor wouldn't cry again. If her sister wanted to be just like her, as she kept saying she did, she'd have to toughen up.

AFTER A HUGE DAY working on the orchard, Wilma had singlehandedly made her family a huge dinner of roasted meats and vegetables, mixed-greens salad, and an assortment of cheeses. Levi loved his cheese and so did Ada and Samuel, and also Fairfax, who had helped out that day thanks to the Millers granting him a day off after he'd done the early-morning milking with Mr. Miller and the others.

When Caroline stopped talking about how odd she found things in the community, Fairfax started talking about orchards. "When I was working at my parents' orchard, we found we couldn't compete with some of the others so that's why we considered doing things differently."

"Like what?" Levi asked.

"*Jah,* I'd be interested to know too," Samuel added.

Cherish sent Hope a pointed look. She should tell Fairfax he shouldn't be giving his ideas to Levi. It was a waste. It was like casting pearls before swine. That thought almost made her giggle aloud, comparing Levi to a pig. Fairfax should be talking to Carter and Florence about his ideas. Hadn't Hope told Fairfax that Levi had been considering selling?

"We never carried it out, but we were close. I had the idea of having people come to the orchard and pick their own fruit, with one of us there to make certain they didn't damage the trees. Our orchard was small enough to do something like that."

"*Jah,* I've heard of it. I've been somewhere they do that," Ada said. "On the way out, their fruit would be weighed and they'd pay for it. And on the way in, their empty boxes and baskets were weighed and labeled, and then the weight of the containers was subtracted out at the end."

"That's right," Fairfax said. "We had cherries, peaches, pears, plums, and apples. The problem was my mom was more interested in the horses and showing them. Then my dad lost interest and just wanted to get to Florida to get my mom away from horses and focused on him."

"So, Fairfax, your idea is to have people pick their own fruit?" Levi asked.

"Basically. Give families the experience of coming into the orchard. It would be the full harvest experience. The season would begin with our cherries and then the peaches and plums. Pears and apples would come later. Then my other thought, which was something we never did, was to dry the fruits and sell them that way."

"*Jah,* we used to do that. Now we just can them and sell preserves," Hope said.

"There are so many things we used to do that we don't do now," said Favor, trying to be part of the conversation. Normally, she just sat there while everyone else talked.

"We need to reassess things. Maybe we should do what was done in the past. I came here thinking I'd improve things, but maybe some things haven't gone

---

the way they should've. And I'm not saying it's anyone's fault."

"You've done your best," Ada inserted. "And that's all we can ask for."

"We don't need to talk about it now, but there will be some changes."

"Cherish, I have a surprise for you," said Ada with a smile. "Wilma told me how upset you were about the *shul* children not being available to come this year."

"*Jah,* I was a bit upset. Disappointed."

"I found a small school who'd love to have a class of theirs come next week. It's a small private school and it'll only be a group of twenty, if you'd like them to come."

"Oh, Ada, I'd love that. *Denke,* so much." Cherish got out of her seat to hug Ada. They hadn't always gotten along, and Cherish was touched Ada had gone out of her way to do something for her.

CHAPTER 25

A BUSY WEEK of harvesting flew by for the Baker-Bruner family.

Cherish was exhausted. She was busy packing up in the late afternoon, after the school children had been and gone. A car caught her eye, turning off the road in front of the house and proceeding onto their driveway. She walked over, wondering whether it was one of the children's parents or perhaps one of the teachers come to see if there were any leftover jackets or other belongings from the children, things that hadn't been picked up when they'd gotten on the bus.

She walked over to meet the person and a young man opened the car door and got out. Right away, Cherish could see his dark suit was crumpled.

When he smiled at her, she forgot all about what he was wearing.

"How do you do?" he asked.

He was handsome, but he talked funny. "How do I do what?" Cherish asked.

He laughed. "I'm sorry. Someone told me I should greet people that way. It sounded weird in my head too."

She put a hand to her head. "Oh, I'm sorry. You mean, how are you today, or something like that?"

"That's right." He stepped forward with his right hand outstretched and she had no choice but to shake it. "My name is Daniel Withers and I'm a reporter."

Cherish took a step back. "'I'm a reporter?' I mean, *you're* a reporter?"

The young man's lips twisted with amusement. "That's right, Ms. Baker. Is that correct, that your name is Baker?"

She gave a tiny nod and said, "Cherish Baker."

"Well, Cherish, I'm a reporter, but don't worry. You look worried."

"I am."

"I just wanted to ask the owner of the apple orchard a couple of questions. Who would that be?"

"Well if you ask my stepfather, Levi Bruner, he would tell you that it's himself. It's yet to be proven."

Daniel's eyebrows drew together. She wasn't sure if it was indicating confusion or curiosity. He waited for her to go on.

Cherish fixed her hands on her hips. "The owner of this place is either my mother or my stepfather. My mother would never talk to you, so your best chance is with my stepfather anyway. What did you want to question him about?"

"We're just doing a human-interest story. It only needs to be half a page."

"About the owner of the apple orchard?"

"About the orchard, really. Unless there's something else around here that's newsworthy … hmm?"

Cherish stared at him. "No, believe me. There's nothing happening around here."

"The editor of the newspaper saw quite a bit of interest from what was posted online."

"And what was that?"

"I'll show you." He pulled his phone out of his pocket, tapped and scrolled through a few things, tapped on a couple of other things, and then he held it out to her.

What she saw was what Caroline had said she'd deleted. "Oh, that's not good."

He shoved the phone back in his pocket. "That depends which side of the fence you're on. That piece has gotten so many views, and I did some digging around, some questioning. I found the profile of the girl who made the original post. From her info, I see she's staying at your apple orchard."

"Oh no." Cherish covered her mouth. This was dreadful. They'd all get into terrible trouble. Especially Favor, because she was the one who had brought Caroline into the house.

"Sorry. I can see you're upset."

Cherish sighed. "It's okay. I'll see if my stepfather wants to talk to you. I'm guessing not. It's nearly dinner time, so I would say that it's no use."

"Please try. I need this story."

"I'll do what I can, but don't get your hopes up. Wait right there, don't move."

He put his feet together and straightened his back. "Yes, Ma'am."

Cherish had a good look at the man before she headed to the house. When she opened the front door, she ran straight into Wilma. "Eek! *Mamm*, you gave me a fright."

"I was just coming out to see who you were talking to. Who is that man?"

"I'm a reporter." Cherish slapped a hand to her

forehead and giggled. "I don't know why I keep saying that. He's a reporter."

Mamm's jaw dropped open. "You must ask him to leave."

"I did, but he wants to speak with Levi."

"What about?"

"About the orchard or something. He said it's an interest story or some such."

"It won't be an interesting story because your *vadder* won't be talking to him."

"Step-*vadder,*" Cherish corrected her mother. "The reporter seems nice enough. Are you sure Levi doesn't want to talk with him? Where is he?"

"He's washing up, getting ready for the evening meal and you should do that too."

Cherish shrugged her shoulders. "Okay. It doesn't bother me. I'll just tell him to leave."

"You should've done that in the first place. You're wasting time dillydallying about."

"I've been working hard all day with the children. Taking them on tours of the orchard."

"Playing, don't you mean?"

"*Nee,* children are such hard work. My neck is aching from looking down at them all the time and my arms are aching and my—"

"You don't need to tell me about that. I had three

of your father's children to raise and then the six of you arrived."

"You were blessed nine times, *Mamm.*" She turned around and walked down the three front-porch steps with the young man watching her all the while. She lifted her hands in the air when she got closer. "I'm sorry. No one will talk with you."

He lowered his shoulders looking completely deflated.

"I'm sorry," she repeated.

"Me too." He reached into his pocket and handed her a business card. "Here. Just in case they have a change of mind."

"Yeah, well, that's something they *don't* do a lot of."

"Yeah, same with my parents." They exchanged sympathetic smiles. "Bye." He opened the car door and put one foot in, and then froze. He looked back at Cherish. "You've got my number. Call me." Then he got the rest of the way in and closed the door.

Cherish watched him leave. Did he mean for her to call him? Just as Cherish was wondering if the man was interested in her personally, and whether he'd meant he wanted her to call him so they could go on a date, Levi swung open the front door.

"Where is he?" Levi's voice boomed.

Now she had to put up with a disgruntled Levi. "It's alright, he's gone now. And I can't be held to blame that he came here. He politely asked if he could interview you and when *Mamm* said to tell him no, and then I said no to him, he left. See? There's no problem."

Levi didn't answer. He walked over to her and looked down the driveway at the car disappearing onto the road. "I would've talked with him."

Cherish could scarcely believe her ears. "You would've?"

"Jah. Why not?"

"Because *Mamm* said you didn't want to talk to him." She held the business card out to him.

"I would've." Levi snatched it from her. "I'll take that. Why don't you go inside? Your *mudder* would want you to help with getting the dinner on the table."

Cherish walked to the house. It was so unfair how she had to work all day and then help with the dinner. Levi worked all day and then he didn't have to help with the dinner. And how was she going to get Daniel's phone number now? She couldn't ask Levi for the card back or he'd be too suspicious.

As soon as Cherish walked into the house, she heard someone in the kitchen with *Mamm.* Good. She didn't need to help then. Too many cooks spoiled the broth, she'd heard. Instead, she slipped up the stairs. She was just about to head into her room when she heard crying. Stepping back into the hallway, she heard it was coming from Favor's room.

She opened the door and saw Caroline sitting on the bed, crying. Favor was doing her best to console her with one arm around her shoulder.

"What's wrong?" asked Cherish, closing the door softly behind her.

"She's upset because she's sure she'll be sent home, now that this reporter's shown up."

Cherish sat on the floor in front of them. "You overheard?"

"*Jah*. We did."

Through her tears Caroline told Cherish, "I did delete it, I really did, but once it's up, it's there."

"I told everyone that's what I'd heard. As usual, no one listens to me. Don't worry about it, Caroline. I don't think Levi's too cross with you. I just had a nice talk with him and he didn't mention you once."

Caroline sniffed. "He didn't?"

"No. I think if you keep quiet and don't make a fuss, no one will be bothered by you. I'm guessing you can stay as long as you want. It might be a good idea to help in the kitchen, too. Maybe offer to do the washing up tonight."

"Nice try, Cherish. It's your turn to do the dishes tonight," Favor said.

"Oh, is it? I didn't remember."

"I don't mind doing jobs around here as long as I don't get sent home. I'm starting to like it here."

"Levi's distracted. He's going to talk with that reporter, I'm sure of it."

"He is?"

"Well, he's going to call him, which is the first step onto the slippery slide."

Caroline inhaled deeply, and heaved a sigh. "I feel so much better. Thank you, Cherish."

And, so did Cherish. She had someone to take her turn for the washing up. Maybe having Caroline stay a while would have its advantages.

CHAPTER 26

A LITTLE LATER, over dinner, Levi was looking particularly pleased with himself. Cherish guessed that something was going on. "Did you call that reporter?" she asked him.

"Jah, I did, Cherish. He's coming back tomorrow evening before dark. He just wants to ask me a few questions. Of course I won't have my photograph taken. I told him that and he didn't mind." Levi smiled.

Wilma stared at him. It seemed it was the first she'd heard of it. "You're going to talk to him? About what?"

"He said it was just a general story about the orchard. I don't see any harm in him asking me a few questions."

"I'm surprised."

Cherish asked, "Because he didn't tell you?"

Before her mother could answer, Levi said, "I didn't see any need. I'm telling you right now." His grin turned into a disgruntled snarl.

Mamm said, "I told Cherish to send him away."

"No harm done, was there?"

"Well, probably not, but I had no idea that you would talk to a reporter. We don't deal directly with the public now, but since now we're talking to the newspaper, we need to think about doing everything different."

Cherish held her breath as tension filled the room. Wilma had never spoken out like that against her new husband.

"I think there needs to be some changes around here. You're right, Wilma. The girls have been saying for a long time that we should be opening that little shop again. I think they're right. It's sitting there empty."

"*Nee,* it's being used as a store room," Favor said.

"I know, but I said empty because it's not bringing in any money. And I know you girls told me that we should do it and I didn't listen to you, and for that I am sorry, but having the shop on our premises here is a good thing and it's silly not to use it."

"We've been saying that forever," said Hope.

"Stop it now, please," Bliss said, in defense of her father.

"I do have a lot on my mind all the time, girls, and it's hard to think about so many things at once. It's not easy being a father, and someone who owns an orchard when I haven't been born into it."

"Yes, I can see it can't be easy for you," Hope said.

"*Denke,* Hope. Don't be too hard on an old man, Cherish."

"*Nee.* I'm not hard on anybody. I'm the softest person you'll ever find out about." Everybody laughed and Cherish looked at them all and didn't know what they found funny. "Well, I am."

"I didn't mean for you to feel bad for *Dat,*" Bliss said.

"I don't feel bad, so don't worry about that." Cherish looked at Levi. "So you're going to tell the reporter that we are going to open our shop again?"

"It seems like a good time to announce that."

"I think it's a *wunderbaar* idea," said Wilma. "For next year, though, not this one."

"Next year?" Hope asked. "Why don't we start

now? We definitely have enough products. We have so much that we could sell."

"We can start as soon as everybody is ready," said Levi.

Everyone clapped their hands.

"Goody."

"I can hardly wait."

Levi looked at Wilma. "I'm sorry, I normally would've talked about it with you first. Are you okay with what we've decided to do?"

"Of course. You don't always have to talk with me about things. I agree with whatever you say anyway."

Levi gave her a smile.

THE NEXT AFTERNOON, Cherish was waiting for the reporter.

When she saw his car coming up the driveway, she alerted Levi that he was there.

"Cherish, make us a pot of tea would you?" he asked.

"I will." Cherish smiled to herself. Daniel didn't look like a tea drinker. She could normally pick what beverages people drank, and she pegged him as a coffee drinker. She couldn't say why, he just seemed like he was a guy who preferred coffee.

"Cherish, get your dog, will you?" Levi called out from the porch.

She looked out the window and saw Caramel jumping all over Daniel as he got out of his car. She hurried out to grab the dog. "Caramel, Come!" Caramel walked over to her and she grabbed his collar.

"Hello again," Daniel said as he walked toward her. "Charity, isn't it?"

Cherish was devastated. He didn't like her at all if he didn't even remember her name. "Cherish."

"Oh, I'm so sorry, Cherish."

"Don't worry, people often get my name mixed up."

He walked into the house and Cherish let go of her dog's collar and then followed Daniel through the door. Once back in the kitchen, she saw her mother already had the hot tea nearly made.

Cherish grabbed a tray and started loading the tea items onto it.

"I'll take it out to them," *Mamm* said.

"No need, I'll do it."

"I want to sit and listen."

"So do I," Cherish said trying to push her mother

out of the way, but this time her mother didn't want to be pushed.

"Stop it, Cherish. I said I'll take the tray out."

"But Levi asked me. You know what he gets like if you don't do exactly what he says."

"Nonsense. He won't care who brings out the tea. You were just there, that's why he asked you."

When her mother grabbed the tray from her, she couldn't do anything about it. She just stood there and watched her mother leave the room.

Cherish was stuck. If she were to go out there and then Levi asked her to leave, she'd be utterly and totally embarrassed. She didn't want to be belittled in front of the reporter. Now all she could do was listen to the interview.

Just when Cherish got herself into a comfortable position on the floor just inside the doorway, Hope opened the back door and walked into the kitchen. She stopped and stared at Cherish. Wide-eyed with surprise, Cherish put her finger over her lips and scrambled to her feet. She ran to Hope so she wouldn't say anything too loudly.

"The reporter, the reporter is here now," Cherish whispered.

"I forgot that was happening. How's it going?"

"It's only just started. Come and listen."

"Mr. Bruner, how did it come about that you own an apple orchard?"

"My wife's late husband was the one who started it. When I married Wilma, she wanted to leave the orchard and make a new start at something else. I wanted to try my hand at something different and convinced her we could make a go of it. I've done many things in my lifetime, but I'd never owned an orchard before."

"And how have you found it?"

"Challenging. I never knew how complicated apples could be. There has been a lot to learn."

"What varieties do you have here?"

"Fuji, Golden Delicious, and my personal favorite, the Honey Crisp. They're the main varieties we have."

"Love the Honey Crisps, too. Tell me what your year's been like. How much work is the harvest?"

"That's two different questions," Levi said. "Which shall I answer first?"

"Any one you'd like."

"Let's see then. This year we started to harvest last week. We'll be four months working from dawn to dusk with the minimum of work done on a Sunday, of course."

"Speaking of Sunday, does your faith disadvantage your orchard?" Daniel asked.

"No."

Wilma asked, "Are you here to talk about our faith or the orchard?"

"Well, I …I'm just interested in Mr. Bruner and his orchard. Do you sell direct to the consumer, Mr. Bruner?"

"We used to, and will do so again. We already have a little shop on our property that we'll be opening again next week. We do sell some apples from there, but it's mainly our apple products. Like apple butter and applesauce, cider, taffy apples and so on."

"Who's going to work in the shop?" Hope whispered.

"Sh. Let's listen," Cherish said. "He has been talking about it."

When the interview was over, Cherish walked out and saw Daniel's tea was hardly touched. "Daniel, I should've asked you if you'd like a coffee? We do have a lovely drip-filter coffee maker here. Would you like one of those, extra shot?"

He smiled at her. "That's exactly how I have my coffee every morning, but at this late hour I don't have any coffee in case it keeps me awake."

"I totally understand." She proceeded to load things onto the tray.

"Well thank you, Mr. Baker, Mrs. Baker, and Cherish Baker."

"It's Bruner," Levi told him. "Mr. and Mrs. Bruner."

"Oh, I'm so sorry. I got confused because it's Bakers Apple Orchard."

"Baker was my late husband's name," Wilma said.

"Yes, I know. I apologize. I'm sorry to have forgotten that. Don't worry, mistakes like that won't be in the article."

"You got *my* name right. I'm Cherish Baker."

"Well I'm glad I got one name right." Daniel laughed.

Cherish walked the tray into the kitchen. While she was in there, Levi escorted the reporter out the door. Cherish was pretty sure that Levi and *Mamm* didn't know anything about Caroline's video that had gone all over the internet. They certainly would've had something to say about that if they'd known.

"He's gone," Cherish mumbled to herself when she saw his car moving away.

Hope and Cherish made themselves busy chopping up vegetables for the evening meal. Then Wilma walked in.

"How did it go, *Mamm?*" Hope asked.

"Good, good. Levi might tell you more about it over dinner. Where are the other girls?"

"I'm not sure. I had to cycle home and I've not been home long."

"I've been here all day. Haven't seen anyone. Don't worry, they'll be here for dinner."

"Are we opening the shop again, *Mamm?*" Hope asked.

"I think so. You'll have to ask Levi."

Cherish had to stop herself from rolling her eyes. *Everything around here these days needs Levi's approval,* she thought. He was the newcomer to the family and it seemed so unfair that he had the final say to everything and kept everybody's money. Still, she had to keep such thoughts to herself. Sometimes she didn't feel like she had one friend in the world. She couldn't talk to her sisters or they would open their big mouths and blab and she'd get into trouble. Her oldest sisters were married, Hope and Bliss had boyfriends, Favor couldn't keep a secret, her only friend in the world was her dog, Caramel.

Realizing her best friend had gotten little attention of late, she slipped outside to find him. She found him lapping water from the horse trough by the barn. "There you are."

She sat herself down on the grass nearby and he walked over to her, and lay down with his head in her lap. She stroked his soft fur and immediately felt better. "Time's whizzing by. It won't be long before we can leave and live on our farm. Things are getting weirder here. No one's said anything about Caroline going home. She's been here for two weeks already. Levi said he wants to sell, and now he wants to open the shop again. He just doesn't know what he wants."

When she heard a noise, she looked behind her. It was Levi. And, he'd heard everything. She jumped to her feet dislodging Caramel from his comfortable spot.

"I won't sell the orchard. We'll all make a full effort. No more outside jobs. We'll all work within the orchard or selling the fruit in stalls."

All Cherish could do was look at him. Now was not the time to say she wanted to keep her job at the café, and Hope would definitely want to keep her job at the bed and breakfast. "Okay."

"Wilma said there'd be more than enough to do if we make the dried fruit again, and sell that as well as the preserves and jams."

"And our apple pies."

"All of it," Levi said.

"I like the idea." That was what they should've done in the first place.

"I've turned down a solid offer on the orchard."

"You have?"

"I got it in the mail today. I don't know who it was from."

"How can that be?"

"It was through Eric Brosley. He said a friend of his was interested. I'm going to write back and tell him the orchard is not for sale. We'll make it work."

"Good."

Levi smiled at her and then turned and headed to the house.

FOR DAYS, Cherish had a bug in her head that she couldn't shake. Who was the true owner of the orchard? When a man died, everything went to his wife, didn't it? Then, did *Mamm* actually, legally, pass everything on to Levi?

Surely there would be some deed to the orchard. A deed of ownership.

The only time Cherish could truly be alone in the

house and not be interrupted was if she stayed home from the Sunday meeting. To do that, she'd have to pretend to be sick, but not sick enough that someone else had to stay home to look after her.

Maybe a simple headache would do …

It worked. Cherish had the 'headache' from Saturday afternoon to make it believable. Then on Sunday she was alone. As soon as she saw the horses and buggies leave the house, she headed to *Mamm* and Levi's room. She knew the bottom drawer in the old chest of drawers was where all the family paperwork was kept.

She waded through birth certificates, old *schul* reports, old letters. Then she got side-tracked reading romantic letters between her mother and her late father. It seemed *Dat* had been truly in love with *Mamm* and she wasn't just a woman he'd married to look after his three *kinner*. That made Cherish happy.

Then she came to the bottom of the drawer. She looked around helplessly at all the old yellowed papers surrounding her. Not one of them mentioned the orchard.

Cherish gathered all the papers and put them neatly back in the drawer, as close as she could to how she'd found them. Then she stood up and looked around the room.

"Where would you keep something important, Wilma?"

She opened the wardrobe and pushed the hanging clothes apart. There was nothing on the bottom there except shoes. Then she spied the top shelf. She dragged the chair in the corner over and climbed onto it. After she pushed prayer *kapps* out of the way, she spied a carved wooden box in the back corner.

She grabbed hold of it, hugging it in one arm as she climbed down, and then sat on the bed with it.

Taking a deep breath, she opened it. There were more yellowed papers. She opened the first one and saw it was a tax notice for the orchard. The next was the same, and the next. Then at the bottom was an envelope. She picked it up, pulled out a folded sheet of expensive-looking paper and opened it.

Her eyes couldn't believe it.

She'd found her father's will.

Then she went on to read that the entirety of the land and dwellings that encompassed the Baker Apple Orchard had been left to Florence Baker.

The will went on to say that Wilma and their children, and Earl and Mark—he named each one of his eight children besides Florence—could reside in the house for as long as they wished. If they worked on the orchard they were to receive fair wages.

Why hadn't this will been enacted? And why did Levi think the orchard was his?

Wilma was named as the executor. The will had been drawn up by a lawyer from a law firm in town.

Cherish carefully folded the will and pushed it back in the envelope. The orchard rightfully belonged to Florence, and *Dat* had made sure that none of them would be homeless. He had known that Florence would do right by everyone.

But, had he known Florence was going to leave the community, would he have made that decision?

Leaving the envelope on the bed, she placed the box back in the cupboard and dragged the chair back to the end of the room.

Then, she grabbed the envelope.

Carter has to see this. He'll know what to do.

This small piece of paper from the past could turn all their lives upside down.

She ran out of the house with the will firmly clutched in her hand.

THE NEXT BOOK IN THE SERIES

Book 12 Amish Mayhem

Find out what happens when Mr. Baker's will is revealed.

Has Wilma been keeping secrets from her new husband?

THE AMISH BONNET SISTERS

Book 1 Amish Mercy

Book 2 Amish Honor

Book 3 A Simple Kiss

Book 4 Amish Joy

Book 5 Amish Family Secrets

Book 6 The Englisher

Book 7 Missing Florence

Book 8 Their Amish Stepfather

Book 9 A Baby For Florence

Book 10 Amish Bliss

Book 11 Amish Apple Harvest

Book 12 Amish Mayhem

For a full list of Samantha Price's books visit:

www.SamanthaPriceAuthor.com

ABOUT SAMANTHA PRICE

USA Today Bestselling author, Samantha Price, wrote stories from a young age, but it wasn't until later in life that she took up writing full time. Formally an artist, she exchanged her paintbrush for the computer and, many best-selling book series later, has never looked back.

Samantha is happiest on her computer lost in the world of her characters. She is best known for the Ettie Smith Amish Mysteries series and the Expectant Amish Widows series.

www.SamanthaPriceAuthor.com

Samantha loves to hear from her readers. Connect with her at:

samantha@samanthapriceauthor.com

www.facebook.com/SamanthaPriceAuthor

Follow Samantha Price on BookBub

Twitter @ AmishRomance

Instagram - SamanthaPriceAuthor

Made in the USA
Monee, IL
17 February 2020